CHEERFUL WEATHER
FOR THE WEDDING

Persephone Book No 38
Published by Persephone Books Ltd 2002

Reprinted 2007
and as a Persephone Classic 2009

First published 1932 by The Hogarth Press
© The Estate of Julia Strachey
Preface © Frances Partridge 2002

Endpapers taken from a 1932 design
for a printed dress fabric by Madeleine Lawrence for
the Silver Studio © MoDA, Middlesex University

Typeset in ITC Baskerville by Keystroke

Printed and bound in Germany
by GGP Media GmbH, Pössneck
on Munken Premium (FSC approved)

ISBN 978 1 906462079

Persephone Books Ltd
59 Lamb's Conduit Street
London WC1N 3NB
020 7242 9292

www.persephonebooks.co.uk

CHEERFUL WEATHER
FOR THE WEDDING

by

JULIA STRACHEY

✳✳✳✳✳✳✳

with a new preface

by

FRANCES PARTRIDGE

PERSEPHONE BOOKS
LONDON

PREFACE

****

Julia Strachey taught me friendship. She was born in India, where her father, Oliver Strachey, worked for the East India Railway Company. 'I adored my Papa and was deeply in love with my mother' she wrote; her life was 'a perfect paradise' until she was five when, after her parents' separation, she was sent back to England to be parcelled out among relations. She came as a boarder to my little country day school; it was recommended by my mother, a friend of the Strachey aunt who looked after Julia, and it was arranged that Julia would spend every Sunday at our house. We would sit in the stable loft and talk about everything. We were eight and nine years old (I was a year older than Julia) but we would talk about free will and free love. We had lovely times together.

When I was fourteen I went to Bedales, where Julia had already been for a year. I did not see much of her because unfortunately a year's difference in age mattered a great deal; I can remember being a prefect and having to tell her to do things. She was not academic and disliked games, gym, cold baths and 'the Bedales spirit'. We drifted apart and I went to Cambridge while Julia lived in Chelsea and attended the Slade. In 1924 she moved in to a room in her father's house at 42 Gordon Square in Bloomsbury; when, in 1926, I came to live next door with Ralph Partridge, our old friendship was quickly renewed.

Julia was unfortunately a misfit in life. She expected a great deal of attention from men and was very flirtatious, yet she was aloof. But somehow she did not antagonise people, they liked her very much. For example, Rosamond Lehmann tried hard to behave well with Julia when she flirted like mad with her husband Wogan Philipps.

Her behaviour may have been because she was abandoned by her parents. After she was five she saw her mother only very occasionally; she had a son but Julia only met him once. There is a story about Julia's father running into her mother, who was called Ruby, and saying, 'Oh, Ruby, you've done well very well for yourself, how many husbands have you had? Three is it?' 'Four, Oliver, four.'

Julia married Stephen Tomlin (whose mother was portrayed as Mrs Thatcham in *Cheerful Weather for the Wedding*) in 1927 but was not really in love with him. The marriage lasted for four years and then Julia lived in a small house in Weymouth Street which Ralph and I also lived in when we were in London. She had many admirers but very few of her love affairs endured. 'However, during these interim years between her two marriages, she flung herself into social life, both bohemian and aristocratic, country house parties and dinners alike, accepting nearly all invitations, and going wherever she was asked,' I wrote in my 1983 book *Julia*.

Cheerful Weather for the Wedding was written at Julia's aunt Dorothy Bussy's house La Souco at Roquebrune On a visit here with Julia years later I wrote in my diary: 'Julia never forgets that *Cheerful Weather* was written here – the one place where life was run on oiled wheels and there were no obstacles to her writing.' It was published seventy years ago, in September 1932, with a dust-jacket designed by Duncan Grant. 'Virginia Woolf had asked Carrington to undertake it when she visited her at Ham Spray on the eve of her suicide, and to do some illustrations, thus proffering her a small interest to go on living, but in vain. The little book struck an individual and tragi-comic note which was recognised by many critics. The *New York Times*, for example, wrote that "this witty little sketch shows evidence of quite unusual humour, observation and insight." After its appearance the literary editor of *The New Yorker* wrote to Julia saying he would publish anything she cared to send him. (It was even said that her book was for a while obligatory reading for his staff)' (*Julia*).

In 1939, while Julia was attending drama school with the intention of learning about theatrical production before writing a play – always one of her great ambitions – she met Lawrence Gowing, the future art critic; he was seventeen years younger than her. One of the first things he told her was that he had read *Cheerful Weather for the Wedding* some years before and enjoyed it very much. Julia wrote: 'I dare say I remember this because it turned out afterwards to be a whopping lie.'

She was very happy indeed with Lawrence Gowing during the next thirty years, for fifteen of which they were married. They roared with laughter at each other's jokes and he looked after her devotedly. From 1962 onwards, after Lawrence fell in love with a very charming and attractive girl, a teacher at the same art school where he taught, they tried for a while to live as a threesome. But sadly, after Lawrence and his new wife had children, this was no longer possible, even though Jenny Gowing was very kind I think and behaved in a very civilised way, and Julia grew more and more lonely.

Julia was amazingly slim and pretty and in the 1920s was for a time a model at Poiret. She had a sharp eye for detail and everything was very vivid to her, her fiercely mocking streak meant that she could be very funny. A wonderful writer, she took her writing very seriously. But she was a perfectionist. I wrote in my book: 'Her highly critical nature (typical of the Strachey family) persuaded her that she must always aim at the highest standards, that it was in fact immoral not to do so, but when circumstances were too much for her then it was better to throw her hand in, and not aim at all.' Everything she wrote had to be good, and it was. When I went through her papers I found many, slightly different copies of the same piece.

'Julia had, I think, a vision of herself as entangled in a web of intransigent practical circumstances created by what she liked to think of as a hostile Cosmos. Getting up in the morning, shopping, being on time – disagreeable molehills to most people – were almost unscalable mountains to her, nor do I believe she fully realised their ubiquity' (*Julia*).

In her diary Virginia Woolf called her 'a gifted wastrel'; Julia was then only twenty-three so this was percipient. But when Virginia read *Cheerful Weather for the Wedding* (published by her and her husband's Hogarth Press) she called it 'a very cute, clever, indeed rather remarkable acidulated story . . . I think it astonishingly good . . . It's extraordinarily complete and sharp and individual – I had no notion it would be so good.' Then she added, 'But I feel she may tear it up at any moment – She's so queer: so secret and suppressed.'

I wrote in 1983: 'Julia reserved her energies for things she really loved doing: she read selectively and remembered what she read, she adored animals and could watch them by the hour, but once told me she "respected them too much ever to keep one as a pet"; she was fascinated by human character and subjected her friends to a piercing searchlight; she revelled in the country but craved the stimulation only found in town. The chief stars in her galaxy were Chekhov, James, Proust and Groucho Marx; her favourite adjectives of praise were "stylish", "scholarly", "creative" and "sophisticated"; those of disparagement "unharmonious" – but also "wholesome", "golden-hearted" and "natural".'

In 1978 Penguin reissued *Cheerful Weather for the Wedding* in one volume with Julia's 1951 novel *The Man on the Pier*; she was not, however, well enough to take pleasure in this. Philip Toynbee in the *Observer* called *Cheerful Weather* 'the slightest but the more perfect' of the two novels; 'the observer is so sharp-eyed and so delicate-tongued that her book reveals, on one level, the rich absurdity of the participants, on a deeper level the helpless despair which they carry about with them.'

At the end of her life Julia lived in Percy Street and her life was lonely and sad. She had moments of clarity and sense but was too ill to take any interest and really lost her way.

****

I would often go and walk to the neighbouring shops with her. I remember going to the hospital in Paddington to see her during her last illness. I was her friend until the end of her life.

Frances Partridge,
London, 2002

CHEERFUL WEATHER
FOR THE WEDDING

****

ON March 5th Mrs. Thatcham, a middle-class widow, married her eldest daughter, Dolly, who was twenty-three years old, to the Hon. Owen Bigham. He was eight years older than she was, and in the Diplomatic Service.

It had been a short engagement, as engagements are supposed to go—only a month, but Owen was due out in South America at the end of March, to take up a post there for several years, and Dolly had agreed to marry and go out with him.

Owen and Dolly were married from the Thatchams' house in the country. (Owen's parents had a house in that part of the world also, —the other side of the sea bay of Malton.)

At the beginning of the wedding morning it was grey and cold.

It so happened that at five minutes past nine, Dolly, on her way through the drawing-room to breakfast, ran into Millman, the middle-aged parlourmaid.

" So sorry, Millman."

" Not at all, Miss. Look, here is something Lily found of yours, pressed down behind one of the drawers in your old bureau that used to be in the old nursery."

Millman handed Dolly a square blue leather bag, faded yellowish in streaks, and with the leather handle swinging loose.

" It must have been there ever since last summer, Miss, when you moved all your things out, you remember ? And the bureau was put up in the attic."

" Good gracious me, Millman. I expect there are all sorts of precious things inside it. Hundreds of lost cheques, my brooch, and that wretched gold thimble of cook's I lost, perhaps."

" Well, you have a good look, Miss. I'm sure I hope you'll find all the lot of them in there! "

Millman laughed merrily and went out of the drawing-room.

Dolly sat down at a small writing-table just beside her and opened the bag. It was all but empty. A layer of grey fluff and something like biscuit crumbs lay along the bottom, and besides this there was a pink bus-ticket and a folded-up

6

old envelope in her mother's writing. She opened the envelope and pulled out her mother's letter. It was dated last July, and the address at the top was that of their cousin Bob's house at Hadley Hill. (This cousin Bob's full title was Canon Dakin. As Dolly's father was dead, and there were no uncles, it was he who was to give Dolly away at the wedding that afternoon.)

Dolly glanced at the letter. It seemed to be a very fair specimen copy of all her mother's other letters.

She smiled, and began to read the letter through : " We had such a nasty wet wk-end for your Aunt B., but K. and Ch. and Mr. F. and P. all turned to and helped her write out her cards for her M.W.O.S. next Sat. and were a very cheerful busy little party. Would you mind filling up the enclosed p.c. and sending it off to L., letting her know if you ever received the address you wanted and that she sent you ? I had lunch with her today and she is so terribly afraid that you never received it as you did not write and thank her for it. Today we have come down to stay with cousin Bob at his new house at Hadley. —Such a cheerful little house right on the top of

H. Hill; rather draughty perhaps, but such a cheery cosy little place for the fine weather! All the flowers look so gay, and there is such a pretty view of the little old Saxon church. We are five miles here from Dinsbury, $7\frac{1}{2}$ from Churton " [" Now we're off," thought Dolly], " only 10 from Great Broddington (8 from little Broddington), and 15 from Bell-Hill. C. and M. also the P. and W. McGr's came over from L. and we went for a nice M. drive. If you drive along the Dinsbury Road from here and bear round to the left by Tiggicombe, and cross the main London and Hadley Rd. and bear up well to the right you get to Wogsbottom, which is only $2\frac{1}{2}$ miles from Crockdalton (and not above 3 from Pegworth) . . ." Dolly skipped the next half-page and began again lower down : " It is such a trial for Cousin Bob that ' K ' will drink so heavily,—they tell me such dreadful stories about him. Of course to me all this seems such a pity! So curious of him! with such a *devoted* mother and father. . . ." Dolly looked up from the letter. She seemed to fall into a kind of trance,—maybe thinking of her dipsomaniac cousin "K"—as her mother called him— who used often to come and stay with her when

they were both children, or maybe thinking of
the main London and Hadley Road.

Above the writing-table where Dolly sat was
an ancient mirror.

This mirror was rusted over with tiny specks
by the hundred, and also the quicksilver at the
back had become blackened in the course of ages,
so that the drawing-room, as reflected in its
corpse-like face, seemed forever swimming in an
eerie, dead-looking, metallic twilight, such as is
never experienced in the actual world outside.
And a strange effect was produced :

It was as if the drawing-room reappeared in
this mirror as a familiar room in a dream re-
appears, ghostly, significant, and wiped free of
all signs of humdrum and trivial existence. Two
crossed books lying flat, the round top of a table,
a carved lizard's head on a clock, the sofa-top
and its arms, shone in the grey light from the sky
outside ; everything else was in shadow. The
transparent ferns that stood massed in the window
showed up very brightly, and looked fearful.
They seemed to have come alive, so to speak.
They looked to have just that moment reared up
their long backs, arched their jagged and serrated

9

bodies menacingly, twisted and knotted themselves tightly about each other, and darted out
long forked and ribboning tongues from one to
the other ; and all as if under some terrible com-
pulsion ... they brought to mind travellers' de-
scriptions of the jungles in the Congo,—of the
silent struggle and strangulation that vegetable
life there consists in it seems.

To complete the picture, Dolly's white face,
with its thick and heavily curled back lips, above
her black speckled wool frock, glimmered palely
in front of the ferns, like a phosphorescent orchid
blooming alone there in the twilit swamp.

For five or six minutes the pale and luminous
orchid remained stationary, in the centre of the
mirror's dark surface. The strange thing was the
way the eyes kept ceaselessly roaming, shifting,
ranging, round and round the room. Round and
round again ... this looked queer—the face so
passive and remote seeming, and the eyes so
restless.

The light perhaps caught the mirrored eyes
at a peculiar angle, and this might have caused
them to glitter so uncomfortably, it seemed
even so wildly—irresponsibly,—like the glitter-

ing eyes of a sick woman who is exhaused, yet feverish.

" I can't understand what the maids are thinking of this morning—a quarter past nine and breakfast is not ready yet ! They keep the meals behindhand in this way—so funny of them ! " exclaimed Mrs. Thatcham, who had come into the room behind Dolly's back, and was running round from chair to chair thumping down the cushions and fluffing them up again. She spoke this in tones of cold amazement, her wide-open eyes sparkling like twin glaciers.

" Well, you'd better hurry along and ask cook for *your* breakfast, dear child, at any rate. Or we'll never get you dressed and ready in all your nice things . . . run along will you, dear child ? "

Dolly threw letter, bus-ticket, and leather bag all together in the waste-paper basket, and made off for the breakfast-room.

Mrs. Thatcham remained behind for a few minutes rushing round the room on tiny feet, snapping off dead daffodil-heads from the vases, pulling back window curtains, or pulling them forward, scratching on the carpet with the toe of her tiny shoe where a stain showed up. All this with a look of sharp anxiety on her long face as usual,—as though she had inadvertently swallowed a packet of live bumble-bees and was now beginning to feel them stirring about inside her. She stopped and looked up at the clock.

" I simply fail to understand it ! " burst from her lips.

She trotted briskly out of the drawing-room in the direction of the kitchen.

II

By twelve o'clock the long hall at the back of the Thatcham's house, where the family was accustomed to sit, was swimming in brilliant sunlight. Also a howling gale had arisen, as usual, for the house was on top of the cliffs. The wedding was to be at two o'clock (the church being just the other side of the garden wall, which was handy).

Sunlight fell in dazzling oblongs through the windows upon the faded wistaria on the cretonne sofas and arm chairs, and lit up the brass Indian tray on trestle legs piled up with magazines and library books. The yellow brilliance was reflected

12

back from the white-and-brown Serbian embroidery hanging on the end of the piano, and from the silver photograph frames, and Moorish paper-knives. And the light of the big log fire was quite eclipsed,—the flames were all but invisible in all this brightness.

Mrs. Thatcham always kept a great number of potted flowers growing in this room, daffodils, fuchsias, hydrangeas, cyclamen. To-day, besides these, a massed mountain of hyacinths, pink, red, and washed-out mauves of all sorts, stood on a table close by the fire, the steely-blue spring light from the window glittering upon each of the narrow waxen petals.

Thrown out full length on the sofa lay a schoolboy cousin of the bride's, aged thirteen— the black-haired Robert—reading *The Captain* magazine. Robert had eyes that were lustrous as two oily-black stewed prunes, or blackest treacle, and the complexion of a dark-red peach.

Padding up and down in front of the staircase, with something pompous and uncanny about his tread somehow, was Tom, his elder brother.

Tom was fair and pleasant to look at, but at

present his blue-china eyes were bulging out of his head like a bull-frog's.

Both boys had just had their hairs brushed neat as satin, and both had changed into black spotless coats for the wedding.

"Robert."

It was as if a big bubble had suddenly risen from the bottom of a dark water-tank and burst, low and hollow, upon the surface,—there was nothing about the slow padding figure of Tom to indicate that it was he who had spoken.

"Robert." (Another bubble burst, low and hollow.)

"Robert. Robert." All the while Tom kept up his padding backwards and forwards.

"Robert." Now the word came softly from behind the sofa-head, Tom having padded round there unnoticed by his younger brother.

"Robert," repeated Tom softly. "Robert. I say, Robert. Robert. Robert."

Tom leant over the sofa-head and chanted softly, articulating his words very precisely, as hypnotic doctors do:

"YOUR MOTHER WOULD UNDOUBTEDLY DESIRE THAT YOU SHOULD RETIRE UPSTAIRS TO YOUR

BEDROOM, ROBERT, IN ORDER THAT YOU MAY
CHANGE THOSE IMPOSSIBLE SOCKS."

There was no sign of life from the patient.

"CHANGE YOUR SOCKS, ROBERT. DO NOT TAKE
ADVANTAGE OF YOUR MOTHER'S ABSENCE TO
PLAY THE CAD, ROBERT."

Robert's black shoes sticking up on the arm
of the sofa were crossed one over the other, and
revealed a gleam of emerald between the shoes
and the trousers.

"Robert. Robert. Robert."

Robert dashed *The Captain* to the ground and,
jerking his head up towards Tom, shouted, "Shut
up, you bally idiot, Tom, will you?" There were
tears in his voice. "What *right* have you to
keep on bullying? You're an infernal, blithering
bully! . . ." And snatching up his magazine he
started reading it again.

A minute passed in silence. Then Tom said
briskly:

"Robert, your mother would desire you to go
upstairs instantly to take off those bounder's
socks, Robert, and to change into a respectable
pair. Will you go, Robert?"

"What the blazes do you mean? I have just

changed into a respectable pair of socks, I tell
you!" cried Robert, jerking his magazine away
in front of his face, and added, "Go and put your
head in a bag."

He gave a gulp and went on reading.

"THESE ARE NOT PROPER SOCKS FOR A GENTLE-
MAN TO WEAR AT A WEDDING," said Tom, bending over the sofa.

"Go and put your head in a bag," murmured
Robert.

Tom paced slowly away across the springy
carpet.

"Would you keep *your mother* waiting——"

"Oh, go and put your head inside a bag!"
said Robert.

There came a piercing shriek from a female
voice half-way up the staircase.

"Lily! Go instantly, Lily, I tell you! Go along!
Go now! Go!"

Someone came clattering down the stairway.

"Go to the sewing-room immediately and tell
Rose she is to find that brooch for me within five
minutes!" and Kitty, Dolly's younger sister,
bounded down into the hall.

She was a big, bold-looking girl of seventeen;

16

her hands, red and much swollen, perhaps with the cold, looked somewhat like raw meat chops appearing from the delicate yellow gauze sleeves of her bridesmaid's frock. Kitty's big face was powdered so thickly over the cold skin with white rice powder, and then rouged so strongly on top of it all, that she almost looked to be wearing a pale lilac blotting-paper mask, with red-ink stains dashed in upon either cheek.

"Oh, Tom, oh dear, oh dear, I know you are thinking that I look utterly and unspeakably stupid and altogether abominable and dreadful in my frock and wreath," she cried out, making for the looking-glass.

"Not at all. Very charming indeed," said Tom, bowing stiffly.

"Yes, you do! You do! I know it well. Why bow in that extraordinary fashion? LILY!" she screamed aloud suddenly, "send that brooch down immediately! Everybody is dressed and ready for lunch!"

A far-distant voice floated down the stairway: "I can't find it, Miss. . . ."

"Yes, you can!" thundered Kitty. "Go fetch Rose, I tell you; don't be such an owl!"

17

"Really, Kitty, I don't think I can bear it!" said a voice from the drawing-room doorway. "Don't you think you could go upstairs and talk to them from up there perhaps?"

A small, neat young lady appeared smiling in the drawing-room doorway, her fingers in her ears. It was little Evelyn Graham, a schoolmate and bosom friend of the bride's. Over her yellow bridesmaid's frock was a grey squirrel fur jacket, and her face was muffled up to the ears in a fluffy woollen scarf. Her narrow green eyes danced and gleamed, and all colours of the rainbow seemed to be reflected in them.

"Br-r-r-r-r, I am more dead than alive!" said she, coming over to the fire, and with horror in her voice. She chafed her thin hands together rapidly, then knelt down and held them out to the blaze.

"You are like a dear, elegant little fly," said Kitty, watching her with a passionate look, and at the same time winding up the gramophone handle. "I wish I were as chic and intellectual as you! *You* must think *me* a kind of great clumsy block-headed rhinoceros in my bridesmaid's frock, I know! Oh, don't speak about it, please! I do beg you!"

"Tut, child, nonsense," said Evelyn. "Oh, what will it be like standing in that draughty church!—Without a coat on! Holding a sopping-wet bouquet of flowers! Really, these quaint old customs are no joke after all is said and done."

"Quaint old . . . oh . . . really . . . Evelyn!" said Kitty, shocked. "Ah, but one of these days you will be married yourself, and you will see! You will be talking quite differently . . . you will make a most wonderful mother, I know. And so will Dolly, too,—in spite of all the things you two say nowadays. . . ."

"Tut, child. Tut," said Evelyn. "Good gracious, what is that?"

A metallic whistling pealed suddenly out of the mouth of the gramophone. It continued, and presently took shape and became a trifling little tune. Tigers seemed to be growling sulkily within the machine also, and it seemed that something like a hyena was faintly laughing too.

Kitty strained her yellow gauze cape tightly round her hips and began darting rapidly here, there, and everywhere, all over the hall in a twinkling, doing some kind of a dance. Her shoulders she held hunched up by her ears. The dance she was performing seemed a mixture between a Scotch reel and a dreamy waltz, for though her legs twinkled briskly like forked lightning all about the floor, yet her body above them seemed perpetually gliding round and round and leisurely revolving, at one and the same time.

"Oh, for Christ's sake stop it, Kitty!" cried Robert from the sofa, staring at his cousin with his glossy brown cow's eyes." You make me absolutely giddy."

"Lily!" screeched out Kitty with all the full force of her lungs, and with a last dart she switched off the gramophone. *"Bring . . . that . . . brooch . . . down here immediately!"*

Her three companions screamed and put their hands over their ears.

The glass garden door grated and was burst open from outside. A violent gale rushed all round the room. Curtains jumped out and off their rods nearly. Something screeched out "R-r-r-r-r-r-r-r-r!" on a long, virulent, piercing wail from under the passage doorway, and everyone's heart turned over in their chests with a feeling of dismal foreboding.

The big hall carpet reared up its head and undulated softly all along its length, like an angry sea-serpent.

"*Milles diables*," muttered little Evelyn, slewing her mouth sideways in a demon's grimace, and she turned up her coat collar.

Mrs. Thatcham walked in, and shut the door behind her, a rough red cloak thrown over her satin wedding-clothes.

"The tortoise has poked its nose out into the world again," she said, wiping her little feet briskly on the door-mat, "in order to bid a last fond farewell to Dolly, I suppose. I think she'll miss that tortoise as much as any of us." A door slammed somewhere down the passage.

"I think she will," said Evelyn.

The tortoise had been given to Dolly by a young man friend of hers—Joseph Patten (a student of anthropology at some college in London)—the summer before.

Joseph was, as a matter of fact, sitting alone in the next room that very instant. He had come down for the day from London.

"Half-past twelve already!" said Mrs. Thatch-am. She stared round the hall with her clear, orange, glassy eyes. "Has Dolly gone up to dress yet?" she asked, with a haggard look at Kitty.

"Oh, she has been up there untold ages, Mum," said Kitty. She was busy in front of the mirror arranging her wreath. "Mum, do you think I look too exceptionally stupid in this get-up?" she asked.

"Half the family not turned up, and the wedding at two!" said Mrs. Thatcham. "We had better (all of us who *are* here) go upstairs and have something to eat. I told Millman to put a cold snack-luncheon up in the nursery, just for the family." She pattered over to the windows, and began pulling back the chintz curtains and puffing up the cushions on the window-seats.

"Oh, such a beautiful day for Dolly's wedding! Everything looks so cheerful and pretty, the garden looking so gay. You can see right over across to the Malton Downs!" She bustled over to the library door behind the sofa.

"Oh, but what is this?" she cried in dismay. She had opened the library door, and there, laid out on a long table, were dishes of cutlets in pale

22

jelly, big salad bowls, bottles of white wine, piles of sandwiches, and so forth. "Oh! But then Millman must have laid the snack-luncheon in here!" she exclaimed.

There was a silence. Mrs. Thatcham stared frigidly at the cutlets and sandwiches.

"How disappointing of Millman!" she said. "She is an odd being, really. So funny of her to do that now! When I told her most particularly the nursery . . . as we shall want the library kept free . . . so very odd of her!"

"Not odd at all, Mum. Considering I heard you tell her most particularly yesterday, at tea-time, to be sure and put the cold lunch in the *library* so as not to have to light a fire in the nursery today."

"Oh no, my dear child. You are utterly wrong, I assure you," said her mother briskly. "I particularly said the nursery . . . never mind, we will all come along in here now, as it is laid. Robert, dear boy! I don't think those great boots look very well upon my nice sofa cover. . . . Come along now and have something to eat, dear child; you will make yourself sick lying upside-down there in front of that roaring fire. Is that a nice

23

magazine—*The Captain*—you are reading? I rather thought your mother preferred you not to read magazines during the holidays. . . ."

Robert sloped in behind Mrs. Thatcham to the library. Tom, seeing him disappearing, took three strides and caught hold of Robert by the elbow, in the middle of the doorway.

"My dear man, you have jolly well *got* to go off and change those socks! Why—suppose, my dear chap, that another man from Rugby should be present at the ceremony! Such a thing is possible, you know!"

Robert tried to wrench free of Tom, but Tom only held him the tighter.

"And just think what that man will say when he gets back to school, Robert! Why, it will be all over the shop! It is terrible! Terrible!" He shook Robert's elbow. "For God's sake go and change before it is too *late*," he hissed through clenched teeth.

"These are perfectly good socks, my dear man. I fail to grasp what you are talking about," said Robert. "Go and put your head in a bag."

Robert shook himself free and made off towards the lunch table.

In the silent drawing-room, that opened out of the hall, Joseph Patten sat on alone.

The light here, that filtered in through the conservatory with its myriad leafy ferns in pots upon wire stands, was turned to a brilliant green.

Joseph might have been a statue in some green stone, dressed up in a tweed suit, sitting there upon the sofa—his light hair, face, mouth, eyes, wrists, and hands were so motionless, and so green.

Kitty floated into the drawing-room on her way through to fetch her mother's rye biscuits from the dining-room.

Joseph caught hold of her yellow gauze cape as she passed him. "Isn't Dolly nearly ready to come down *yet?*" he asked, for the sixth time that morning.

"I don't know, I'm sure," said Kitty, and floated away through the twilight.

Joseph walked into the family hall, and stood pressed up against the glass garden door looking out over the terrace.

Little Evelyn Graham put down a magazine she was looking at upon the brass table, and went and joined him there.

25

A kind of brassy yellow sunlight flooded all the garden. The arms of the bushes were swinging violently about in a really savage wind. The streaked ribbons from a bush of pampas-grass, immediately outside the door, streamed outwards in all directions. This bush remained squashed down as flat as a pancake to the level of the gravel terrace in a curious way, and it looked unnatural, as if a heavy, invisible person must be sitting down on top of it.

"Have you observed," began Evelyn with a giggle, "that Mrs. Thatcham's one criterion of a beautiful day is whether or not it is possible to see across as far as the Malton Downs? 'Can you, or can you *not*, see across to the Malton Downs?' —that is the only question. For the farther you can see,—why, the more beautiful the day! And not the day only, either, for the beauties of the landscape, and the countryside also, hinge entirely on the answer to that question."

Evelyn sniggered, and continued, warming to her subject: "Thus, if it is possible for Mrs. Thatcham to see *two* counties at once from the top of a hill, then the view from there is a fine one,—the country exceedingly lovely. If *three* counties are visible at the same time, it is then more lovely than ever,—the country-side positively magnificent; and so on and so forth."

The young man gave half a smile, and turning his head farther away from Evelyn, continued staring silently out of the glass door.

Evelyn glanced up at his averted face, then immediately left him and went to join the others in the library.

Joseph, when satisfied that he was alone in the hall, sat down on the sofa, beside the hyacinth table.

Five minutes later Millman, carrying a tray of whisky and soda, halted on her way through into the library.

"Not feeling very well, sir? Would you like me to bring you a drop of brandy? It's sometimes rather a good thing if you are feeling a little bit seedy or anything."

"No, thank you."

"Oh, very well, sir. But there's plenty handy if you should want some," and she passed on.

In the end he got up to go and join the others in the library.

As he passed the red baize swing-door into the passage, it opened, and he found himself close up against a tall, grey-haired man, in black clerical clothes, with a gaunt white face reminiscent of a Pre-Raphaelite painting of Dante. It was Canon Dakin, or Cousin Bob of Hadley Hill as the family called him.

Shaking hands with Joseph with ceremonial politeness, the Canon proceeded along to the library beside him, questioning him cordially as to how he was getting on with his studies in London.

Joseph, blushing a deep red, and smiling, broadly the whole while with embarrassment, answered his questions, walking unsteadily along beside the Canon sideways—as a crab walks, stumbling up against the corners of sofas, and of pianos, as he came upon them—as it were from behind, each time. Mrs. Thatcham had said in cold surprise once, walking behind Joseph and Dolly down to the bathing-place: "That young man seems to be walking *backwards* instead of forwards. I really can't imagine how he ever gets anywhere! Such a very quaint person! . . ." She disliked Joseph. It seemed to her that he said

28

deliberately disgusting and evil things in front of her young daughter Kitty; in front of the servants too: he very often wounded her feelings; and altogether she experienced a feeling of anxious strain when he was in her presence.

Canon Dakin and Joseph took their places at the snack-luncheon table, where they found that a red-haired cousin, a young man of twenty, nicknamed "Lob," had already joined the family party.

"Hey! Here comes the Anthro-pop-ologist!" shouted Lob, waving his fork in greeting (he treated this science completely *de haut en bas* always).

"How are your lectures going?" asked Kitty of Joseph, a kind of desperate intenseness in her voice and face. This was her style of the moment with the male sex.

"Very well, thank you," said Joseph, and added: "We heard about the practices of the Minoan Islanders upon reaching the age of puberty at the last one." He started snapping up his cutlet.

"Oh, really? How *terribly* interesting!" said Kitty.

"Yes, very. Like to hear about them?" offered Joseph.

"Kitty, dear child! Kitty! Kitty! Open the window a trifle at the top, will you! The air gets so terribly stuffy in here always!" cried out Mrs. Thatcham very loudly.

"We have seen Two Men who are willing to Throw the Bones with reference to Heaven!" recited Lob, pointing his fork upwards into the air, and rolling his *r*'s sonorously.

What he said was merely one of the many passages he had picked up out of Joseph's anthropological textbooks, and which he was fond of reciting aloud at odd moments, and without any apparent rhyme or reason.

Mrs. Thatcham called across to Kitty over at the window: "Bring me that lamp-shade lying on the window-seat there! I'd like to show everybody! It is a wedding present from Dodo Potts-Griffiths, just sent over by the chauffeur. She made the whole thing entirely herself, painted it, put it together, and everything, and it really is so very cheerful and pretty!"

Kitty came back with the lamp-shade. It was a parchment cube, whipped all along the sides with plaited thongs of leather, which gathered themselves together into long tassels depending from the bottom rim at each corner. At the bottom of each tassel hung a knot of discoloured wooden beads—purple and yellow, and some marbled stone ones, and some tiny elephants and monkeys also. On the parchment shade itself was an Elizabethan galleon. Above and below the galleon (forming two bands round the top and bottom rims of the lamp-shade) were heart-shaped leaves.

The galleon and the leaves were not, in any sense, painted from Nature, yet they were not exactly diagrammatic either. Rather it was as though an average had somehow been arrived at of all the Elizabethan galleons and of all the leaves that had ever before been painted on a lamp-shade, and a diagram then drawn to represent this average.

The galleon was tinted rust colour and orange. For the leaves, it seemed that the artist had mixed together one-third blue paint, one-third green paint, one-third dust—and filled in the outlines with this mixture.

"Now, do you not think this is quite wonderful!" cried Mrs. Thatcham, holding the shade out to the Canon, and with the look of agony on her face which always accompanied her expressions of admiration for an object. "A wedding present for Dolly! So nice!" she cried shrilly. Her face was drawn long as a fiddle-stick. "I really think this is such a nice cheerful pattern she has painted up round the border here! Vine leaves, I suppose . . . aren't they?" She was peering with tense anxiety at the leafy border. "Oh no, though! They cannot be vine leaves! For these are heart-shaped . . . perhaps they are periwinkle leaves." She put on her pince-nez and devoured the pattern rabidly through them from under knitted eyebrows. "Yes! Why, that is what they must be! —periwinkle leaves—how wonderfully clever!" She withdrew her pince-nez abruptly from her nose.

Everyone gaped at the painted lamp-shade held up in Mrs. Thatcham's hand.

There was the sound of a cat's sneeze, and every eye swivelled round in the direction from whence this sound had proceeded.

Joseph, with head bowed over his plate, was quivering violently from head to foot, and every now and then sneezing like a cat—at all events that is how it sounded.

The company soon understood that the young man was attacked by a fit of the giggles, and all looked surprised; excepting Evelyn, to whom giggles and laughter were as water is to a fish. And so, although not understanding very exactly what was the matter, she joined in now with Joseph immediately.

The young man, apparently unaware that the whole table was watching him, kept on shaking his bowed head hysterically, as if flies were bothering his ears; kept hitting his palms softly against the sides of his chair, quivered from head to foot, and bounced up and down on his seat all the time as though riding in a jolting taxi. All this in silence, except for the quick bursts of cat's sneezing.

All of a sudden he tossed up his flushed face boldly and shook the straggling locks out of his eyes with a free gesture. But immediately he seemed to bounce high up off his chair again, and to come down with a bursting sneeze a hundred times more violent than all before.

"Somebody seems amused enough about it at

any rate," said Mrs. Thatcham. She picked up the black horn salad spoon and fork, and conveyed a quantity of cubed potatoes and beetroot in mayonnaise on to her plate.

Joseph raised his head, tossed back his locks again, and, throwing out his arm with a lordly gesture, seized the silver salt-pot and swept it through the air to his plate, where, with very free-hand gesturing, he swung showers of salt out of the little perforated silver lighthouse down upon his cutlets, with wide rotating swoops some two feet in diameter.

"And what do *you* think of Miss Dodo Potts-Griffiths' present?" Evelyn asked him, her narrowed eyes reflecting the sunlit greens of the garden outside the window.

With two quite weak sneezes Joseph seized upon the water-jug and wafted it up and down above his tumbler (like a well-bucket rising and dropping), pouring out a thin stream of water all the time as he did so.

". . . Oh! . . . the lamp-shade?" said he all of a sudden in a startled voice. He shook some loose strands of hair off his forehead. "Well, it is certainly a most skilfully contrived expression, and

34

gratification, of the herd instinct—I must allow that—and, as such, a really most appropriate gift for a wedding." He popped a thick crust of bread into his mouth, munched it voraciously and, stretching out his hand, caught hold of a giant bowl of trifle, to which he helped himself pretty liberally.

"Disappointing!" said Mrs. Thatcham, and drew in her breath with a loud hissing sound. She stretched out her round middle-aged arm for the lamp-shade. "Miss Griffiths doesn't seem to have found very much appreciation for her talents and arduous labours *here* at all events." Her breath hissed again, as she drew it in between her almost shut teeth. "Lob, dear boy, are you all ready for the church, I wonder. The ceremony is at two, you know! I want you all to be in your places ten minutes beforehand. Of course, it always much amuses me to hear you young things discussing the experienced and skilled labours of women of the world—old enough to be your grandmothers—who have been practising their talents since long before *you* were first rocked in your cradles. However; s-s-s-s-s-ssh-sh-s-s-s. Pass your plate along for more trifle, Tom. I

35

really *cannot* get over our good fortune in having such wonderful weather for the wedding!" She sat back, very upright, in her chair, twisting her thin gold bracelets round upon her left wrist, and stared unwinkingly across at Joseph with a blank orange eye.

His little fit was now completely over. While it lasted it had been ecstatic and whole-hearted; and now, like a sparrow that gets up out of its dust-bath again, after having fluffed about all over the place with care-free frenzy for three or four minutes, he set to work once more pecking away at his food wherever his eyes could best light upon it.

And now what many of the younger members of the family had been dreading happened. Aunt Bella, an unmarried sister of Mrs. Thatcham's, arrived among them.

"So the animals are being fed in the library!" cried Bella, stepping in over the threshold. She laughed heartily, and for some minutes. Aunt Bella's flowered grey lace dress and floating scarf showed up her cinnamon skin and black eyes to advantage. Her diamond earrings which flashed and sparkled and swung about, her grey snakeskin vanity bag, shoes and gloves, seemed new and expensive, and reminded one of shop windows. Her eye wandered round the room of young people as she seated herself in the window. There were not enough chairs to go round now, and the younger ones of the family rose to their feet and wandered uncertainly about here and there nibbling at sandwiches and *petits fours.*

"Oh, I am feeling so wickedly proud of my beautiful new car! You cannot imagine!" she whispered as it were delightedly, and in confidence, to the glassy-eyed Tom, and laughed very heartily, drawing his arm through hers.

"Oh yes? Really?" he answered, and gave a stiff little bow.

"And oh!—I have got such a perfect pet of a chauffeur! You know, Tom," she lowered her voice again, "he simply treats me as though I was —I don't know *what!*—"

"Oh, really?"

"—made of sugar or—or something, that will melt at the least drop of rain! And that must be so wonderfully carefully cherished and looked after!"

37

"Oh no. How delightful," murmured Tom, edging away towards the lunch table.

"I cannot help being really rather touched, (and secretly) profoundly amused by him!" went on Bella, her eye wandering over to the red-haired Lob. She laughed again mischievously and, getting up, went across to Lob.

"Well, Lob! And how are you these days!"

Very soon she was telling him about her staff of servants in her house across the bay; telling him he must come and stay with her over there, so that they could laugh over the whole *ménage* together. "And you know, Lob"—her voice sunk to a whisper—"those three funny old things—the laundrymaid, the parlourmaid, and the cook—have been with me for thirty years. Ever since they first came to me from the village! And oh! they are such very dear, quaint people, —and you know, Lob—though I say it as shouldn't—they simply cherish *me*—I don't know *what*—I might be the Queen of England! Really!"

"My dear lady," replied the cheerful Lob, speaking unexpectedly loudly, and holding his glass of wine up to the light for a moment, "I don't care two pins about all that! No! The question, as *I* see it, is quite a different one. The whole thing is simply *this*: Is it possible to be a Reckless Libertine without spending a great deal of money?"

His Aunt Bella looked taken aback.

The fact was that Lob was inconsequent in his conversation at all times, and to-day he had had the good fortune, before coming across the wine, already to have laid hold of four glasses of best sherry.

"Because," he went on, raising his long third finger, "other things being equal, that is what I intend to be."

"Pray what do you mean—what other things being equal?" asked little Evelyn Graham, who was standing close behind him in her grey fur jacket.

"Ah—ha! Ha! Ha!" shouted Lob, vague and delighted, and bursting into a guffaw of laughter, he wagged his long finger at her archly.

"I am sorry to hear you have formed such dastardly plans for the future at your age of youthful innocence," said Aunt Bella. She looked uneasy. She caught hold of Canon Dakin's arm as he passed her.

39

Mrs. Thatcham called to Lob from her seat at the snack-lunch table:

"I think, dear boy, you had better put down that glass for a while. . . . Why don't you go out and take a turn in the garden? The fresh air will do you good. Go along and show Cousin Bob our beautiful new sensitive plant, down in the lower greenhouse. (Take the boy out into the fresh air, for goodness' sake, Bob, and pray don't let him come into the church in that condition.) Tipsy already. Disappointing!"

Meanwhile, no less a person than the bride-groom himself had appeared upon the scene. There were exclamations of amazement on every side.

Owen was a man who had enormously wide shoulders and a thick neck, like a bull; he had a flushed, simple, affectionate face, although it wore a wary expression at the minute.

"Oh, Mrs. Thatcham, this is too dreadful of me! I know this is the last place in the world I ought to be in at the present moment!" He laughed heartily, but was plainly embarrassed. ''The fact is, Dolly has got the ring! She took it to have it made larger at the jeweller's. She promised faithfully she would give it back to the best man, but—er—ah—er—has apparently forgotten to do so." He looked down, reproachfully, at a tall yellow daffodil that was leaning up sideways out of its pot towards him.

Tom was sent upstairs to Dolly's room to fetch the ring.

The lunch party transferred itself back into the hall. Bella, who had brought over some gramophone records, now put one on the gramophone.

Surrounded by many strange "in-laws" he had not met before, Owen now went round among them all, his face beaming, his white teeth flashing, crying, "Splendid! Splendid! Capital! Oh, capital! Splendid!" all through the room.

Somebody started saying "Hush," and hissing like a snake in order to silence the room for the new gramophone record.

It was Miss Spoon, the girls' one-time governess.

Owen looked frightened, and dropped down instantly on to the sofa to listen.

The record had not been long going before Owen, with an uncomfortable face, began beating time to it. "Ta, ta, tee-ta!" he whispered, marking the time with one finger and looking with an anxious sidelong glance into Kitty's face, as she sat beside him on the sofa.

He leant forward towards her and whispered, "Oh, this is the most capital piece! An old favourite!"

Kitty stared back blankly into Owen's flushed face, which she observed shone steely lilac all down the left side in the bright spring light from the window. There was something miserably guilty and anxious endeavouring to hide itself behind his rigid features.

Tom, who soon returned with the ring, went over and joined his younger brother behind the sofa upon which Kitty and Owen were sitting. And these two soon heard an angry whispering behind them.

"Robert! I beg you—I implore you!—I ask you for one moment to imagine something! Will you, Robert? Listen. You are kneeling there in the church, Robert! The ceremony is in full swing: the clergyman is praying, the church is full of flowers, everybody, *everybody*, is as smartly dressed as they can be, Robert. All of a

sudden you glance up! You see a man from
Rugby staring at you from across the aisle! He
has a curious smile on his face, Robert. And he
is staring. Staring. *Down at your socks——*"
There was a violent scuffle behind the sofa and
Robert dashed suddenly through into the drawing-room.

Tom followed upon his heels, colliding with
Mrs. Thatcham as he rounded the corner.

"What? Never been to Chidworth!" she was
exclaiming to a white-moustached stranger beside
her. "(Dear child, do look where you are running
to, s-s-s-s-sh-s-s-s.) Oh, but you must go to
Chidworth! Why, you can see three counties at
once from there on a fine day! Then the little
village is so pretty! All the little gardens so
cheerful and gay. . . . It is five miles from there
to Waddingchitwold, you know. . . ." As she
piloted her guest up the hall stairway she murmured, "I have arranged for you to go into the
lilac room; you have a rather nice view from
there. . . ."

"The lilac room? Mum, how many more
people are to go into the lilac room?" shouted
out Kitty from below. "Cousin Bob! Mr.

Spigott! Aunt Bella! Miss Spoon!—a pity the
bed is such a narrow one!" But her mother and
her visitor had already disappeared, and did not
hear her.

Kitty flounced off into the drawing-room. She
had seen Joseph Patten disappear in there a
moment or two before. There he was, alone in
the green twilight again; but in a different chair
this time. Now his face looked black viewed
against the glass fern-filled conservatory.

"Mum makes living in this house unbearable,"
Kitty said, and flung herself down in an armchair. "Yesterday, you know, I began really and
truly to fear for her sanity! Well, it is possible
to become unbalanced in advancing years, isn't
it? Mum would ring the bell for Millman: 'Millman! Tell cook to make two extra pots of liver
pâté for tomorrow's sandwiches.' As soon as
Millman had left the room, it was: 'Kitty! run
and tell Millman we will not have the extra *pâté*
after all. We will telephone for more sandwiches
from Gunter's.' Then, later in the day she would
go down and row poor old cook up: 'Cook!! but
where are the two extra pots of liver *pâté*?' 'I did
not receive orders for extra liver *pâté*, Madam.' "

44

"Isn't Dolly dressed *yet?*" interrupted Joseph.

"I don't know. 'I did not receive orders for extra liver *pâté*, Madam.' Then Mum would say, 'Do you mean that Millman forgot to give you the order? Well! She is a curious person really!' and she would hiss at poor old cook through her teeth."

Kitty gave a wild, strange cackle, like a hen who is suddenly caught hold of, and looked up at Joseph.

His face was turned away, and with a large handkerchief he was wiping something off his cheek.

"Aren't you feeling well, Joseph? Oh dear, oh dear, oh dear, I had counted on you as being the one bright spot at this awful family gathering——"

But the young man had risen, and now walked away rapidly out of the room without listening.

"Well, this is all rather gloomy, really!" thought Kitty. "Lob is such an idiot. Evelyn thinks me provincial—I know she does; I know she does; and doesn't want to talk to me. Tom goes snooping round after Robert the whole time, like an octopus after its prey in deep waters

—it really makes one's blood run cold to see them. . . . But perhaps there will be some naval lieutenants later, at the reception." And she fell to picturing manly sun-bronzed faces ranged in a semicircle round her at the buffet, and limpid sea-blue eyes gazing intently into hers. And she began wondering how in the world she was going to keep those limpid eyes from glancing downwards at her swollen hand as it held up her glass ice-platter,—from suddenly noticing with repulsion how huge, coarse, and purple it looked beside the delicate rose-pink pyramid ice. . . oh dear, oh dear, her shameful hands! Why, what bad luck it was really!—My God? What bad luck!

III

Meanwhile the bride-to-be was busy attiring herself for the wedding ceremony.

Dolly's white-enamelled Edwardian bedroom jutted out over the kitchen garden, in a sort of little turret. It was at the top of the house, and reached by a steep and narrow stairway. Coming in at the bedroom door, one might easily imagine one's self to be up in the air in a balloon, or else inside a lighthouse. One saw only dazzling white light coming in at the big windows on all sides, and through the bow window directly opposite the door shone the pale blue sea-bay of Malton.

This morning the countryside, through each and all of the big windows, was bright golden in the sunlight. On the sides of a little hill quite close, beyond the railway cutting, grew a thick hazel copse. To-day, with the sun shining through its bare branches, this seemed to be not trees at all, but merely folds of something diaphanous floating along the surface of the hillside—a flock of brown vapours, here dark, there light—lit up in the sunshine.

And all over the countryside this morning the bare copses looked like these brown gossamer scarves; they billowed over the hillsides, here opalescent, there obscure—according to the sunlight and shadow among their bronze and gauzy foldings.

Within doors Dolly stood bent over the wooden washstand, whitening her black eyebrows with frothy lather, her nose bright pink, and dripping with soapy water. As her face came

47

out from behind the sponge each side, it wore a reproachful, stupefied expression.

All about the airy bedroom, maids of different kinds, in dark skirts and white blouses stooped low and searched about for stockings and garters, or stood warming satin shoes and chemises in front of the coal fire.

On a table in the bay window was a glass vase with a bunch of long-stalked narcissi in it. The flower-heads on their thin, giant stalks were no bigger than sixpenny pieces, and each had a frilly orange centre. One or two red dwarf tulips were stuck in among the narcissi.

Cold puffs of wind from the partly opened window fidgeted all the flower-heads about, and kept up an irritating squeak, squeak, and sharp banging of the loose window-hasp up against the framework. That was unpleasant to the occupants of the room, undoubtedly; but what must have been delicious to them was the fresh, sweet, springlike scent of the narcissi which went wafting round on the air upon each new puff of breeze from the windows.

Dolly finished washing, arranged her black hair with the rust-red strips in it neatly. She dipped something that looked like a limp orange "Captain" biscuit into a pink bowl on the dressing-table, and afterwards dabbed and smeared it all over her reproachful-looking face, leaving the skin covered over evenly with light corn-coloured powder.

The whole toilet was carried out as a performing elephant might make its toilet sitting up in a circus ring,—languidly, clumsily, as though her arms were made of iron.

With Jessop, her mother's elderly lady's-maid, and with her dear friend Rose, the young sewing-maid, Dolly chatted a little, but her voice was like a piano that is played all the while with the soft damper so pressed down that it can barely be heard.

Jessop, dressed in black, with her face as yellow and wrinkled as a grocer's apricot, and with her long nose like an ant-eater's, went travelling round the room on tiptoe as usual, as though she were in an invalid's darkened chamber; and there was now, as always, a pained expression on her yellow face, as though she knew of something very shameful afoot somewhere in the household, which she realised to be none of her business all the same. She moved with a kind of modest majesty, as one imagines royalty must delight to do; and her eyes she kept down-cast upon the carpet.

"I wore my white satin wedding-shoes down to dinner last night, Jessop," murmured Dolly. "And they are grey and soiled at the toes now; isn't it dreadful."

"Tut! Tut! You ought not to have done that, Miss," breathed Jessop, looking a little offended. Dropping her voice, she whispered in confidence, "Never mind, Miss! Give them to me, and we will see what we can do with them. You see, Miss, we have spent many, many years over this kind of little matter, and so you see we know one or two little wrinkles by this time. . . ."

Dolly held up the white satin shoes to her.

"Thank you, Miss," breathed Jessop in a repressive voice, her eyes cast down upon the carpet.

She received the white shoes in her wrinkled claws, and glided majestically away with them to the bay window.

Rose, a very pretty pale-faced girl with thick black eyelashes, usually in the highest of spirits

—a girl who was for ever dropping things on to
the sewing-room floor and ejaculating, "Bang!
There go my false teeth!" and exploding into
peals of laughter—today was looking very
solemn, as she hooked up Dolly's wedding-dress.

"The Princesse Teresa," said Rose, in her
high silvery voice, like a little bird singing (she
named a foreign royalty who had lately been
married to an Englishman and had had her photograph in all the papers). "The Princesse Teresa
had a wonderful beautiful wedding. Didn't she?"

Rose did up the last hook intently. "When
the clergyman asked her, 'Who takes this man
to be their lawful wedded husband,'" she went
on, "they say the Princesse answered up, in such
a clear voice, so that everybody, right away down
to the back, could hear her. 'I DO!' she said."

Dolly glanced at Rose. She found her looking
emotional; and more solemn than she had ever
seen her before.

The woman started to fix the long wedding-
veil on to the pearl coronet that was pointed
like a starfish, upon Dolly's head. The veil, which
had belonged to Dolly's wealthy Portuguese
grandmother, seemed unendingly long and bulky

in the small bedroom. Gigantic billowing fold upon fold of lacy birds and flowers seemed heaped up over the bed, the rocking-chair, the table, and everywhere.

Dolly knew, as she looked round at the long wedding-veil stretching away forever, and at the women, too, so busy all around her, that something remarkable and upsetting in her life was steadily going forward.

She was aware of this; but it was as if she were reading about it in a book from the circulating library, instead of herself living through it.

"Sweetly pretty flowers, aren't they?" said Rose, nodding towards the bridal bouquet of lilies and white carnations that stood in a blue jug of water in the corner.

"Dolly!" shouted a male voice up the stairway.

The door was open. Dolly recognised Joseph's voice. "What! again?" she said to herself.

"Hulloa!" she echoed back, faintly.

There was a silence.

"Hulloa!" she called again, but in her present mood it sounded only as loud as a dying kitten's mew.

Silence again.

"Are you coming down soon?" called up Joseph at last.

"I don't know," she answered. "I'm not dressed yet."

A considerable pause followed.

"Do come down," came Joseph's voice at last.

"Oh, indeed! Pray, why in the world *should* I?" whispered Dolly loudly to herself. Aloud she repeated, languidly, "Well, you see . . . I am not dressed yet."

A long pause followed, and Dolly took it that he had gone away again.

"Will you be finished soon?" presently came Joseph's voice once more.

Dolly waited, and then said, in a careless sing-song voice: "Oh, I don't know at all . . . I'm afraid . . . No, I really have not the faintest notion."

"Well, I will be in the drawing-room," croaked Joseph, but something seemed to muffle his voice this time and Dolly did not catch what he had said. His footsteps retreated down the passage.

Dolly was now dressed and ready for the wedding. She told the handmaids they might go.

When she was alone she rustled in her long skirts over to the bay window and sat down on the window-seat in the sunlight.

Out on the croquet lawn a short figure was standing alone, a scarlet cloak billowing up in the wind behind her. It was Mrs. Thatcham, and she was examining a black dot on the grass at her feet.

Seeing Whitstable, the gardener, with his white Panama hat and yellow waxed moustache, walking along the path between the cabbages below her, Dolly opened the window and shouted down to him.

"Whitstable! Can that be the tortoise come back again? Out there on the croquet lawn?"

"Yes, Miss!" shouted back Whitstable. "Yes! Oh, I knew he'd be somewheres about! I seen him once or twice during the winter season, snuggling up against the glass-house stove-pipe; —and I don't blame him neither."

"Please tell Millman to get the girls to pack him up immediately," shouted Dolly. "I shall take him with me to South America! He will enjoy himself out there much better than in this windy climate."

54

"Yes, Miss." Whitstable trudged off towards the kitchen.

He heard Dolly's voice in waves upon the gusts of the wind behind him: ". . . rye biscuit tin . . . big holes punched in the lid . . . lettuce leaves!"

"Very good, Miss!"

He turned the corner.

Hearing a tap at the open door, Dolly turned her head and saw little Evelyn stepping up warily into the room with a glass of red port wine in her hand. Behind her was Kitty.

The girls came in and shut the door. Evelyn sat down in the rocking-chair.

Dolly quaffed off the wine. "Not that I stand much in need of it," she remarked. She put her plump white hand behind the window curtains and drew out a tall bottle labelled "Jamaica Rum," and showed it to Evelyn.

"You certainly do *not* need it—by the look of things," said Evelyn. She had noticed that the rum-bottle was half empty.

Kitty, who had opened her wide scarlet-lipped mouth to burst out into praise of Dolly's beauty as she sat there in the sunlight in her wedding-clothes, remained with it open, paralysed, upon seeing the bottle.

"Oh! how very, very awful," she said at last. "I couldn't have imagined such a thing possible! A bride sitting upstairs in the bedroom swigging rum!—out of a bottle!—just before entering the church for her wedding ceremony!"

"Really!" murmured Dolly, raising her black eyebrows, surprised. "Well, yes, you've still got a lot to learn, my child, it is true," she added, sighing.

Kitty balanced herself in her yellow satin high-heeled shoes upon the brass fender. "I'm sorry to say it, Dolly," she said, "but in some ways it will be a good thing when you are no longer in the house. It will not be so demoralising for the servants, at any rate."

Dolly gave a weak laugh.

"Well, well, that is a pleasant thing to say to your sister on the eve of her departure for South America," she murmured.

"I admire you and your set frightfully, Dolly!" shouted Kitty, slipping off the fender sharply, and then clambering up on to it again. "I know you are marvellously clever! And interesting! and witty too. But I do think the way you look at certain things is absolutely BEASTLY—there is no other word for it. You know what I mean. . . . And even on your own wedding-day! . . . And there's Joseph down there been saying such stupid, awful things again. . . ."

"What things?" whispered Dolly, faintly.

"Oh, what does it matter. You will only think them funny."

"You must tell us!" said Evelyn.

"Oh, very well then—well—I told Joseph that an Englishman in love lacked poetry . . . that is how it started. I told him about that awful Robinson youth down at Malton: how, when his car broke down as he was bringing me home after a dance in the early hours, and we had to walk up the hill at five o'clock in the morning, instead of looking at the sunrise, or at me, all he could do was to stump along with a face black as thunder, muttering, 'After tonight my name is mud in Malton! My name is mud in Malton!' 'My dear chap,' I said to him, 'really! What *does* it matter *what* your name is in a place like Malton?' I told Joseph I envied Barbara McKenzie her Spanish naval officer, who plays to her on his ukulele in the moonlight, and is not ashamed of his love for her. I'm going to Spain next autumn, by the way, Doll, with Ursula Mac-Tavish and her family, if Mum will let me."

Kitty broke off and examined the heel of her shoe carefully on both sides.

"I told Joseph I thought *he* would play a ukulele beautifully," she added, "and that I couldn't imagine *him* ever being ashamed of his love for a woman,—well! I don't think he *would* be. Oh, well—but he shut me up and became quite ratty for some reason, and began telling me: 'You must know, Kitty, that I don't at all care for all this snobbish Continental talk of yours about foreigners, love, poetry, and ukuleles. You must understand that there are still some of us left who don't appreciate that attitude in our womenfolk. We aren't accustomed to it, and we don't want it. It's un-English. My own aim is still the clean-limbed, dirty-minded, thorough English gentleman, and I still have hopes of being one. Yes, I hope to achieve great things,' and all the rest of it."

Kitty stamped her foot and turned pink. "I *loathe* you all when you start to talk in this way!

. . . An English gentleman is *not* dirty-minded, I tell you! He may lack poetry and be a bit on the stiff side, certainly, but dirty-minded is just what he is *not*!"

"How do you know this?" enquired Evelyn from the rocking-chair.

"How do I know?" shouted out Kitty, slipping off the fender with a bang and clambering up on to it again. "Is Cousin Bob dirty-minded?" (She alluded to the Canon.) "Was *Dad* dirty-minded?"

"Terribly. Terribly," murmured Dolly, looking depressed, her forehead resting on a limp hand, her plump elbow on the window-sill.

"You are drunk!" said Kitty.

Dolly did not deny it.

"Well, anyway, *I* think it is all utterly disgusting!" shouted Kitty, and ran out of the room, her cheeks red and burning.

"I don't mind telling you, Evelyn, that we have been treated to these lectures every single day for the last twelve months now." Dolly poured some more rum into a tooth-glass. " 'Dirty,' 'Clean.' 'English gentleman.' 'Spanish guitar.' The whole house rocks with it. And the worst of it is one suffers a terrible revulsion after a bit, like that time when we were all given boiled cabbage cut up into squares every lunch-time and dinner for a month, do you remember? . . . That miserable Joseph cannot resist baiting Kitty on these subjects." Dolly sighed. "He likes to stir up the wasps' nest a little with a stick, and then run away and hide, and then, of course, the wasps fly straight upstairs and sting innocent people. . . ." She swallowed down the rum. "There has been such a desolating muddle with the Pall Mall Depositories," she went on in a whisper, her forehead piled on her languid hand again, her eyes cast down upon the floor.

"The Pall Mall Depositories! Why!—what has happened?"

"Well, you know old Aunt Minnie died a little while ago."

"What?" said Evelyn.

Dolly's voice was now too soft to be audible. It had been slowly fading away for some time, and in talking to Dolly now, Evelyn felt as if she were trying hard to telephone to somebody up at the Firth of Forth, on a very bad line, in thundery weather.

"... I told you, Aunt Minnie died a few months ago," repeated Dolly in a whisper.

"What? Oh yes?"

"She left several cabinets of curios (if you know what they are) that she had collected, to be divided between Kitty and me."

"M-m-m?"

"Well, Mother made a list out of all the different objects in the cabinets before sending them to the Depository to be stored, in accordance with the Depository regulations. You see, I was busy buying things for South America myself."

There was a silence. Only the hum of the fire burning and the occasional squawk of the loose window-hasp could be heard.

Dolly sighed heavily.

She continued: "It seemed the list did not correspond with the contents of the cabinets. That brute at the Depository—Humble, or Gumble, or whatever his name is—sent back the whole lot of these cases of curios last Friday. With the result that I have been sitting on the cellar floor surrounded by lighted candles, sorting all the objects ever since—old Spanish coins,

E   61

keys, and goodness knows what all, knee-deep around me."

A moan burst from Evelyn's lips. Dolly went on, almost inaudibly: "Mum would pick up a filthy little embroidered Indian bag, eaten away by moths and hanging in ribbons and tatters. 'Now, here's rather a useful little object. I like these nice curly-wigs all over it. I wonder what they used *that* for? I dare say they kept their turban-pins inside them—quite a good idea. I suppose this clip passes through the ring here. But how neat!' and so on, and all the time one's back was aching as if knives were being jabbed into it."

"Oh dear, I am so sorry!" burst out Evelyn. "Why didn't you wire to me to come and do it, dearest? You must be completely worn out, with all your packing to do as well, and——" She looked with dismay at the expression on Dolly's down-bent face. "Oh, how miserable, dearest creature."

Dolly sat with bent head, silent. And Evelyn saw with despair that tears began to splash down on to her white satin knee.

"You are tired, Dolly dear. And no wonder.

How I wish you hadn't drunk all that rum! But that can't be helped now. Cheer up, dearest, you will soon be bathing under blue skies. And then resting in the shade of fanning palm trees."

Dolly blew her nose. "You will faithfully promise to come out and stay with us; won't you?" she whispered. "Owen insists on paying for your passage. (And he can well afford it, I assure you.) I could not possibly exist there for long without you." Dolly gave a hiccough. "Oh, God. Now I've got the hiccoughs. Oh dear. And Owen says no more could he either. Oh! oh dear, oh dear."

Evelyn promised faithfully she would go, and gave Dolly a glass of water to sip.

And now, seeing that it was a quarter to two, and Mrs. Thatcham had made everyone promise that they would be in the church ten minutes before the ceremony was due to begin, Evelyn reluctantly got up and left Dolly.

"Ready, dear child?" shouted Mrs. Thatcham, outside the bedroom door. She had just passed Evelyn upon the narrow staircase.

She came in, rearranged Dolly's veil, stroked her hair once or twice, and kissed her.

63

"I am proud of my beautiful daughter," she said.

On hearing these soft and—as it might be—tenderly playful words, at such a moment, from such a person, Dolly turned sharply away and, with her back to her mother, leant down and began fumbling loudly with the loose and squeaking window-hasp.

"Do go down, Mother dear," she mumbled. "I have one or two last things to finish off. Do go down. I must really."

Her mother hesitated, but when Dolly continued to rattle and thump on the window-hasp and then suddenly burst out (still leaning out of the window), "Oh, blast this bloody thing! Mother, *do* go *down!*"—she bustled away down the staircase after all.

Dolly stood holding tightly on to the window-hasp, the sunlit country outside shivering as a golden, heaving blur through her tears.

She remembered a letter she had received that morning from a certain German lady, a friend who lived in Munich. Half-way down one of the pages her friend had written: "I am haunted all the time by the feeling that my last years are upon me. I *cannot* resign myself to this, try as I may. I love fire, vitality, beauty, and movement in all things . . . and *loathe* sitting still in armchairs, aching all over, one's teeth dropping out one by one. . . . Do, dearest Dolly, I implore you, enjoy yourself as hard as ever you can, while you are still so young and lovely. . . ."

"She is on the wrong tack in this last sentence. I must write and tell her," thought Dolly. "Neither youth nor loveliness makes people happy. It takes something utterly different to do that."

She sat down on the window-seat and began to think, yet once again, of the last summer, spent almost entirely, minute by minute, with Joseph . . . building a summer-house together, floating up and down along the coast in his boat. . . .

"Never a word! Never one single word the whole time!" she suddenly burst out, aloud. She jumped to her feet. Drawing in a long breath she began smiling—if smiling it could be called. "All is well! He does not care for me, and therefore will not miss me!"

The cold wind blowing on her from the window had made her face seem swollen, chilled, and grey and patchy-looking. She went over to the mahogany chest, and, opening the deep top drawer, fetched out a handkerchief, and after a few minutes, "He is an odd fish, all the same! . . ." she muttered aloud in a doubtful voice. She began remembering certain incidents, more especially once at a large dinner party at the hotel in Malton one time. There had been a discussion about a certain kind of crackly biscuit made with treacle, and looking like stiff brown lace, called a "jumbly." "What, never tasted a jumbly!" Joseph beside her had said, quite suddenly, peering in underneath her large summer hat. "But you must taste a jumbly! You would adore them!" But the point was, that through his face, and most especially his eyes, Joseph's whole being had announced, plainly, and with a violent fervour, not "You would adore them," but "I adore you."

(Exactly in the same way that the hero in Tolstoi's story *Family Happiness* turns and speaks to the heroine suddenly of frogs, and she understands, as he speaks, that he is telling her he loves her. Dolly had read that story shortly afterwards.) "Only Tolstoi's hero had not just had an *apéritif* and a couple of glasses of wine, one presumes," reflected Dolly.

"Supposing, just supposing," went on Dolly, "that Joseph came up to me now, five minutes before the wedding though it is, and confessed, at last, that he had loved me all along, begged me to run off with him, by the back door, across the fields, while everyone was sitting waiting in the church for me, now what should I do after all?"

"Dolly!" called up the Canon from the passage. He was waiting below to take her to the church.

"Only five more minutes, you know!" he cried. "All going smoothly?"

Everybody else had left the house by this time, excepting these two.

And also a third: Joseph.

IV

Joseph was standing beside a bamboo table in his bedroom, staring at the white wall-paper covered with its bunches of dark violets tied up with pink twist. His pale cheeks were wet, and he could not stop shivering from head to foot, steadily, like an iron spring which is vibrating.

67

In the turmoil of feelings which had descended upon him, quite unexpectedly, during the last half-hour, and which he was utterly powerless to disentangle or make the least head or tail of, one idea had now come up to the surface at last, and beat like a little hammer all the while in his terrified mind.

"Stop the wedding! Stop the wedding! Stop the wedding! Stop the wedding!" it went.

What for, exactly, he couldn't imagine—but there would be time enough afterwards to reflect upon that. But now! in five more minutes it would be too late! It would be too late!

Suddenly he rushed to the door and flew out of the room, crying "Dolly! Dolly!" in a panic, and ran down the staircase into the hall three steps at a time.

At this moment Dolly was trailing slowy down the back staircase (which was nearer to her part of the house than the main one), her lace train wound round and round her arm. From out of the voluminous folds of this there peeped a cork and the top of the neck of a bottle. In her other hand was her large bunch of carnations and lilies.

At the bottom of the stairway, in the shadows,

Whitstable, the gardener, was waiting for her, his Panama hat in his hand.

"Excuse me, Miss, but could you spare time to step into the kitchen and let my old mother see you afore the ceremony! Half a minute only would suffice, if you could see your way to it. . . ."

Dolly looked anxiously up at the clock and hurriedly rustled through into the kitchen.

Old Mrs. Whitstable was sitting in a farther room, the cook's tiny sitting-room, in a wicker armchair. She resembled the blackish nobbled and twisted stump of an old elm tree very much more nearly than she did a human being. Although she was all but blind, and all but deaf also, and no longer had many wits in her possession, she had set her heart on seeing Dolly (whom she had known from a child) in her wedding-clothes; and Whitstable had accordingly wheeled her along, in a Bath chair borrowed from the blacksmith for the purpose.

"Don't get up, Mrs. Whitstable, please! Stay where you are!" cried Dolly from the doorway, but the old creature had already tottered to her feet.

"Of course, she isn't as young as she were, now, and she do think of you as being quite a little tiny kid, Ma'am. We never can get her to understand, not properly, as how you have growed up into a young lady since her time," remarked Whitstable, as usual.

Interviews between Dolly and old Mrs. Whitstable ran their due course as smoothly as does a familiar gramophone record—not one note ever being varied during the process.

Dolly, who was already markedly late for her wedding, was wondering at what point she was going to be able to remove the needle from the disc, so to speak, this time.

Meanwhile the old lady was droning ahead in a low voice, not much louder than the evening wind playing through a withered holly bush:

"Oh, I remember you, when you come back to me bringing our little doggie Patch in your arms after that motor-car accident. He weren't troubled a bit by it! Not a bit! Saving only just a sore scratch on the end of 'is tail. No need to worry about old Patchy!"

This was her opening speech, always. The dog

referred to had not been brought back to her by Dolly, but by a neighbouring farmer's daughter; and, in fact, the accident had nothing to do with Dolly whatsoever.

"Her memory isn't quite what it used to be . . .," muttered Whitstable here.

The old lady fixed her clouded eyes upon Dolly's white satin-covered knees.

"And now you are growed up into a fine handsome woman," she went on in her sing-song.

"Oh, Lord," thought Dolly, her eyes on the clock.

"And your husband will be a fine handsome man. And you be proud of him, and he be proud of you, and you be proud of one another." (This last speech had often embarrassed Dolly in the past if she had chanced to have a young man along with her whom she was at all sweet on, when she dropped in at the old lady's cottage with some message from her mother. Whitstable would hastily chime in at this point, "She ain't got her wits about her nowadays, Miss!")

Dolly always tried to keep her eyes off Mrs. Whitstable's hands during these interviews, the flesh of which was already black as ebony with extreme age—this blackness of the flesh does not usually occur until after death—and the bones and joints of which, as before-mentioned, were so beknobbed and twisted about as to be literally unrecognisable as human hands at all.

"Of course, I lost my eyesight nowadays," whispered the wind in the holly bush, "and something seems to rise up inside my head all on a sudden and everything turns black and purple in front of my eyes, and I do fall over on to my back on the floor, with the dizziness. Oh, nobody do know! nobody do know what I do feel rising up within my head sometimes! And that come upon me all of a sudden! And I can't fancy nothing to eat now, you know!—only just bread and water, only just bread and water; or if anyone has got a nice rabbit's head or anything, I do enjoy a nice broth out of *that*: I can always eat a broth off of a nice rabbit's head——"

"Well, Mother," interrupted Whitstable, anxiously, "Miss Dolly has got to be going."

"This is the end, fortunately," thought Dolly.

"Well, you be a fine handsome woman, my dear. And your husband be a fine handsome man. And he be proud of you, and you be proud of

him, and you both be proud of one another—
but, Laws! you have shot up something *terrible*!"
she finished off unexpectedly. She was staring
upwards towards Dolly's neck and chin with a
horrified and dumbfounded expression on her
face.

This was quite a new ending for once.

"Oh, she be remembering all the time when
you were nothing more than a little tiny thing,"
explained Whitstable. "I expect she have just
noticed how much taller you be grown." He
turned round as he said this to the retreat-
ing Dolly, but she was already through the
door before he could properly twist his neck
round.

Joseph, meanwhile, hearing voices somewhere
in another part of the house, began rushing
through all the rooms, his face as white as paper,
searching everywhere for Dolly. At last he
bounded up the backstairs, and on, up Dolly's
private stairway, to her bedroom. The door was
open. The room was empty. A pink box of
orange powder lay overturned upon the carpet.
A strong smell of narcissi filled his nostrils.

On the bed, a heap of blue tissue paper kept

73

wafting up and down at the corners in the draught from the open door. The empty, deserted room! What is more deadly depressing?

The clock on the dressing-table said five and a half minutes past two. Maybe she had left the house then? For certainly the ceremony was due to begin at two.

He turned round and tumbled like a maniac down the narrow staircase, and then along the narrow passage to the main stairs.

"Dolly!" he heard the Canon's faint faraway shout to his niece, from down below somewhere.

So she was still in the house! He clattered off down the main stairway. The landing was empty. He ran despairingly, first to the right, into the sewing-room; then to the left, into the nursery; then back and on down the main stairs into the big hall. There, at last, was Dolly.

She was standing in the middle of the hall, her head bent, regarding something black upon the front of her white wedding-dress. She looked up at Joseph, and her face was red as a radish and wore a frantic expression of horror. Her eyes were staring insanely.

74

"For Heaven's sake, what am I to do! What am I to do! I cannot go into the church like this!" she screamed up at him. She held out her skirt towards him; her small hand was dark blue, and upon the white satin was a black stain as big as a tea-pot.

By her toes lay an overturned ink-bottle.

Joseph ran down to her. "Oh, Dolly! Do for pity's sake listen———"

"Suggest something! Suggest something!" screamed Dolly, her eyes flashing. "I know! Run upstairs and get a scarf out of mother's drawer, will you!"

"One moment! Dolly! dearest!"

"Do go! Please don't stop!" shouted Dolly, stamping her foot. "In the bottom drawer! A white lace scarf! Quickly!" And she pushed him away towards the staircase.

Joseph bounded up the stairs. He managed to rout out the scarf from the drawer.

When he came down Dolly was half-way up on the turn of the staircase, to meet him.

"Dolly!" came the Canon's voice sharply from the drawing-room. "You must positively come, my dear!"

"Coming, Cousin Bob."

"Help me tie it round my waist, Joseph, round here, round here," Dolly, with fingers of forked lightning, was fastening the lace scarf so that it hung down and covered the inkstain.

Joseph snatched her left wrist, and clutching it tightly, held it up in the air, a long way from him, as though it were a viper that was trying to dart its forked tongue into his flesh. His face now had changed, seemed to have gone to pieces; it showed strain, and a kind of convulsions upon it, as though some frightful change and combustion were taking place just inside it. His mouth was drawn, and he laboured under a choking in his windpipe.

"For God's sake, tell me one thing," a queer voice was saying from his throat.

"I will tell you anything in the world you like *afterwards*," wailed Dolly, and her wrist wriggled so sharply in his hand that he was obliged to let go of it.

"Dolly! Dolly!" bellowed the Canon.

"Coming!" she shrieked back. "Pin this!"

She shoved something small and knobbled into Joseph's fingers.

He looked down and saw it was a round emerald brooch set in pearls.

"Against the stain, in front of the stain! Oh, do hurry!" wailed Dolly.

Choking, and shaking his head in a gesture of despair, Joseph knelt down to pin the lace scarf over the ink stain on Dolly's skirt.

Staring at the ink-stained stitches of some white flowers embroidered on the satin, he mumbled, "How did you manage to do this?" all the time trying to fasten the brooch.

"I was trying to fix the cork back into my rum-bottle over there on the writing-table, with one hand only—the other was holding my bouquet. The damned thing slipped, and ink-bottle and all fell over on to my dress. Was ever anybody so unfortunate before?" Dolly began laughing hopelessly.

"Dolly!" shouted the Canon.

"Here," cried Dolly, and brushing rudely out of Joseph's hands, she disappeared into the drawing-room. There was a rustling of skirts, and then the door at the far end of the drawing-room banged.

"Well. It is over now," said Joseph aloud.

In scarcely a minute Joseph saw the top of
Mrs. Thatcham's old Sunbeam car gliding along,
upon the other side of the garden wall, towards
the church. He then remembered that he, too,
should long ago have taken his departure in the
same direction.

He sat down on the sofa.

In front of him, hanging over the banisters
crookedly and as though just about to slip down
on to the floor, was a voluminous red Chinese
robe covered all over with a complicated net-
work of creases. The sun from the window
fell on this garment and threw up each crease
into sharp relief. Dim-looking dust fogged
the surface of the cloth all over. Moreover it
all looked sticky to the touch; somehow, altogether the garment looked fusty and repulsive
beyond words.

Joseph leant back against the sofa and heaved
an elephant's sigh.

"Thanks be to Goodness that she wouldn't
let me tell her anything!" he ejaculated. "Who
knows but that she might really have postponed
the wedding!—and what in the world should I
have done about it afterwards!"

The church organ sounded clearly through the hall.

That meant the bride was advancing down the aisle upon the arm of her cousin, the Canon.

v

Joseph, who expected to have the next twenty minutes in which partially to recover himself, upon the sofa, was surprised and annoyed to see the red baize door swing open after only three or four minutes had passed.

There came in a midget of a village woman, like a mosquito, wearing a blouse and a skirt. She wore an enormous apron, but instead of a servant's white cap, she had on a shiny black hat with a few discoloured forget-me-nots fixed up against one side of it. She staggered in under the weight of a deep wooden tray piled up with gilded china.

Panting and grunting, her face round and red and glossy as a polished apple, she put the tray down upon the Turkey carpet, in the centre of the room, under the chandelier.

Going over to the little writing-table, she

79

picked up the red blotting-pad, the pen-holders, the china stamp-box and so forth, two by two, went over to the piano and dotted them all about on top of it. When the writing-table was cleared, she spread an embroidered tea-cloth upon it.

"Oh . . . curse and drat it!" she growled immediately, and, whisking it off, respread it, but with the other side uppermost.

Standing back a pace and staring at her handiwork, she exploded into a torrent of giggles, which made a husky reverberation down in her chest.

Meanwhile Joseph might have been a fly on the ceiling, for all the notice she took of him.

"This is the first time ever *I* fussed round a droring-room tea-table then! Believe me, or believe me not. All them little cakes in jelly and all of it. Oh no! Very decidedly not!" said she, addressing the tea-tray upon the floor.

She trotted out of the room again. She was soon back, carrying a cake-stand and some tea-spoons. When she had rid herself of these, she came over to the middle of the room, and standing with her hands on her hips, addressed the tea-tray upon the floor again.

"The gentleman that come to see about the hot pipes out in the lobby, said to me, '*I* have two of my own,' he said, 'what are both of them big strapping great boys by now. And oh . . . good golly!—what devils and demons they do be!' he said. 'Well,' I said to him, 'my son Teddy is exactly the very same thing over again,' I said. 'All the time this cigarette-smoking, they pointed boots, and all of it, why, devils and demons isn't in it with such as *they* are,' I said. No. Very decidedly not!"

"Will she ever go out of the room again?" thought Joseph.

The little woman stooped down and began taking up the cups and saucers off the tray. "Yes! They come down and asked me if I would help with the wedding teas and all of it. If you ask *me* (now I don't know what manner of a gentleman I am addressing at the present moment—mark me well), but if you ask *me*—well, then in my opinion, marriage is a totally mistaken idea." She breathed heavily and scowled at the teacups in her hands. "My husband has been dead seven years. *Thanks be for that then.* And never no more nothink of anythink of that again for me!"

There was a silence during which the woman got on with laying the tea-cups. The organ started playing again down in the church.

"Go. Go. Go," said a loud voice in Joseph's head to the little woman.

"Teddy came home late last Friday night again," she started, and Joseph saw she was talking to the tea-tray on the floor once more.

"I was lying in bed at the time. Mark me well. He came right in and began the selfsame song all over again: 'Mum, are you going to let me have half a crown this week, please?' 'No, TEDDY. Why should I give you what I up and earn by the sweat of my brow to go merely spending on cigarette-smoking, and the gees, and all of it?— most emphatically I AM NOT.' And he up and emptied a bucketful of cold water over me as I lay. Sopping the bedclothes and everything. 'CURSE YOU, MY BOY,' I said."

"Strange doings!" thought Joseph dimly. He had hardly heard her recital though; he was wondering if he would be able to get a talk with Dolly.

The little creature was staring up into Joseph's face, he suddenly noticed.

"Have you got the face-ache?" she asked.

"The face-ache? Yes . . . I have."

"Oh! I wondered! Oh! Well, you're a gentleman what has got a capital set of teeth, if ever there was one!" she exclaimed, and immediately bustled over to the tea-table. "Now, Teddy was keeping on tying a piece of thread to his tooth all last week. He'd tied the other end on to the door-handle——"

"Here come the people from the church. Look," pointed out Joseph.

She stood up on tiptoe. Sure enough, cars were beginning to glide along the other side of the garden wall, conveying the bride and the guests back again to the house for the reception.

"Oh!" said the little woman. She seemed disappointed.

"They'll be coming in here in a minute," warned Joseph.

"I'd best be getting along then," muttered the little one, uncertainly. She gathered up her tray and left him in peace.

Now the regular wedding crush began—but at the farther end of the house, in the large front drawing-room, and in the study.

One or two of the guests had evidently strayed through into the small drawing-room opening out of the hall, however.

For Joseph heard, in a lady's hushed and cautious tones: "Of course, I know one shouldn't mention such subjects on an occasion of *this* sort, but really!"—here she dropped her voice too low for it to be audible in the hall—"as big as a *cartwheel* ... I assure you! ... and entirely composed of violets ... truly! ..."

"... But how did he afford ...? *Surely?* ..." came in a different, huskier female voice.

"Oh, my dear, but didn't you know?—*umbrella handles!*" hissed the first voice. "Mints of money!" There was a subdued giggle.

"Mrs. Drayton!" This was a third voice, and Joseph recognised it as belonging to little Jimmy Dakin. He was the seven-year-old bearer of the bride's train and youngest son of the Canon. His voice was very low-pitched, deliberate, and slow. "Have you heard this riddle, I wonder?" asked Jimmy.

"What riddle, dear?"

There was a pause.

Jimmy's voice said, "Tell me, please: What is

84

the difference between a honey-*comb* and a honey-*moon?*"

"Good gracious! I'm sure I don't know."

"It is this: A honey-comb has one *million* cells, and a honey-moon has *one*. Rather good, isn't it?"

"What? My dear child! Really!"

"Lily told that one. Good, isn't it?"

"Well, don't go and tell it to the bridegroom, that is all I ask you."

Joseph heard sounds of stifled laughter.

Mrs. Thatcham suddenly pushed in backwards at the baize door, and piloted into the room an aged aunt of hers, whom she settled upon the sofa by the tea-table.

"I had a special little tea put in here for you, Aunt Katie, so as you could be out of the crush. Oh!—*that's* not very nice!" Mrs. Thatcham's eye had caught sight of the stamp-box, pens, envelope holder, etc., studded about over the top of the piano. "Now, why are the writing things on top of the piano? Oh! Why, she must have used the *writing*-table for the tea things instead of the tea-table! Now, how funny of her! Can you imagine her doing such a thing? S-s-s-s-s-s-s-s. So odd!"

"Well, it was mad Nellie up from the village, Mum," brayed Kitty,· who had come into the room behind her mother. "I told you she would make a muddle of everything; look, here's the jam-pot nestling among the scones at the bottom of the cake-basket. Can you conceive of anything more idiotic?"

"Well, you certainly would think she could unfold a tea-table at her time of life. S-s-s-s-s-s-s-s-s-sh-sh. What a very curious person," said Mrs. Thatcham in a tone of reserve.

"The tea looks perfectly delicious, and that is the only thing that matters," cooed old Aunt Katie. "I'm simply *dyin'* for some of that lovely Cape gooseberry jam!"

Aunt Katie was a thin, sly-looking old lady, who sat very upright, and who had round, black boot-button eyes, brilliantly lit up with some very enigmatic expression—whether intense merriment, or malice, or what, it was difficult to decide. She was dressed in three shades of violet, with many slender gold and silver chains round her neck. The nose on her pale astute face was red as a cherry. White lace, finely written all over in loops and squirls with a thin black snaky velvet

86

ribbon, made a yoke to the top of her dress. Her gauze scarf, pink as a cyclamen, and marked like a butterfly's wings, had hundreds of little tucks upon it, and was edged with lace.

Aunt Katie's hats were like Mediterranean gardens in full blossom. Today her hat was strangely wide and flat, and supported along its brim a regular shrubbery of black cherries, purple and scarlet geraniums, yellow speckled pansies, spiky green sprays of something—oats, or ospreys, and heaven knows what besides. Some pallid silvery-pink roses stood up from all the rest, and looked like refined, blonde English peeresses amongst a horde of gipsies. In looking upon their large, crinkled, ashy-pink faces, one felt the cool relief of evening superimposed upon the meridian glare.

Aunt Katie leaned forward. "Are you coming to have some tea with your old Aunt Katie?" she asked little Jimmy Dakin, who stood hesitating, in his white satin jacket and knickers, in the drawing-room doorway.

Jimmy came and sat down by his great-aunt, and the pair began their tea.

"And you took tea with your cousins at Boxbridge last week, I hear," said the old lady, handing the boy a cup of tea.

"I hope your Cousin Roger was nice to you. He is gettin' such a grand person nowadays; captain of his cricket team at school, they tell me!"

Jimmy's face was round, and brown as a hen's egg. He was a tiny little boy. As for his features, they were so small they could hardly be seen, bunched up together as they were in the middle of his face, like the currants in a penny bun when they all run into the centre together for some reason. Two velvety-brown eyes were always on the watch above these tiny features, and if the curious glance of another got caught up for an instant in the beam of their penetrating gaze, they would be lowered instantly, leaving the spectator gazing, baffled, at this very demure, reserved, *comme il faut* brown currant bun.

Joseph, on the sofa, looked in despair at this couple at the tea-table. Impossible to say good-bye to Dolly in any of the other rooms, surrounded by strange people! And now, here in the hall also, was Jimmy and his aunt, and Jimmy eating and talking so maddeningly slowly that it

88

was clear that the couple would be there for a good two or three hours at least.

"Then Roger offered me a plate with some scones on it," Jimmy was saying slowly. "I took one of those. The scone I took was just about the size (just about)—or rather just about the *tallness*—of a whistle."

"What is the tallness of a whistle, my dear?" asked his great-aunt.

"Well, I believe I should have said—just about the tallness of a whistle with a marble laid on top of it, or perhaps a fountain-pen (on its side, of course!) laid on top of a whistle. Well, after I had finished that scone, he offered me a plate of cocoa-nut cakes. 'Oh no,' I said. 'I cannot eat another cocoa-nut cake.' 'Well, then, will you have some bread and butter to finish with?' he said. 'Oh no,' I said. 'I really could not do *that*. No. I cannot eat any more bread and butter.' "

Jimmy's brown eyes kept a systematic look-out over the room as he talked. It was clear that he was only relating his story in order to keep his aunt entertained. "Well *then*, (even *then*) he tried to persuade me to eat something further! He handed me a plate with only one biscuit on it. It

89

was about the size, I should say—let me see now —of the end of that tea-spoon with a bus ticket beside it. . . ."

Joseph sprang up, and opened the door into the library. The library was empty. Quickly shutting the door again, he went off to fetch Dolly.

Aunt Katie stared out of the glass garden door on to the terrace, where a semicircle of bridesmaids could be seen, their yellow dresses whipping up and down in the wind, their hair streaming. Two men in billowing mackintoshes kept running round a camera on a tall tripod in front of them. The whole partly looked more dead than alive.

"Those poor girls must be simply shiverin' in the icy blast! I wouldn't care to have *my* photograph taken in such a costume, on a day like this!"

"B-r-r-r-r," cried Mrs. Thatcham, bursting open the garden door from the outside. "Rather fresh out today!" She rubbed her little feet cheerfully on the mat and bustled through into the drawing-room.

At the same moment, unnoticed by her or Aunt Katie, or Jimmy either, Dolly (dressed now in her dark going-away costume, and looking, with her hair untidied under a jaunty pink velvet hat, a trifle vulgar) glided along the wall behind the tea-table and in at the library door. Joseph was close at her heels.

Joseph shut the library door softly to, behind them.

VI

There was not much light in the library, for where there were no shelves filled with dark leather volumes, there was heavy wood panelling painted chocolate brown, and massive plush curtains shrouded the windows.

The remains of the family "snack lunch" still stood upon the long table. Crumpled-up napkins, and cloudy wine-glasses half filled with yellow wine, stood about higgledy-piggeldy among the bowls of half-finished trifle.

"Why, what is this?" cried Dolly, in a very high, airy, very amused tone of voice, and she picked up a dark mass of material from the wooden window-seat. It was a green tartan kilt and sporran. A rose-pink canvas mask dropped to the floor from out its folds.

Joseph and Dolly looked down at the mask. A pair of square gelatine spectacles with vermilion rims was placed over two goggling blue-china eyes; a frayed ginger moustache and false teeth were sticking out in all directions. To the forehead was fastened a pale blue cricketing-cap.

"Oh, that is just something that Lob and Tom and a lot of them dressed up in, to have their photographs taken," said Joseph.

"Why?"

"Oh, to send to Kitty. Don't let's talk about that now."

There was a pause.

"Why *did* they have their photographs taken in such garments," enquired Dolly in her high, airy-sounding voice.

"Oh, it was to be a practical joke on Kitty. They were each going to send her their photograph with a different inscription underneath, as Kitty's admirers always do, you know: 'To Kitty —because of a glorious afternoon in an orchard at Hove . . .,' and so on—you know the sort of thing Kitty's room is filled with. . . ."

"I see." Dolly sat down on the window-seat and stared out at the garden, her face devoid of expression. When, at length, she glanced up at Joseph, she saw a face the colour of a beetroot gazing meaningly and imploringly at her. She hastily dropped her eyes.

"Have you settled your mother comfortably in up at Liverpool?" she asked.

"Yes."

"And your course of lectures up there,—they take six months, don't they?"

"Yes."

"And you are proposing to go to another set there?"

"Yes."

"And will you really enjoy them—or are you rather dreading the whole business?"

"It will be all right."

"Do you know anybody up there?"

"No."

Dolly felt him looking imploringly at her face.

"But I suppose you will be able to get introductions?" she said.

"Oh, don't let us go on talking like this!" he burst out.

Dolly glanced up sideways. He was blushing

redder than ever, and now gave her a miserable forced smile.

Dolly bit her lip and turned her head quickly towards the garden; her own face now flooded with colour also.

"But, really, though, why not? I seriously do want to know all about it . . .," she said. After a moment she slightly turned her head and gave an uneasy, curious glance at him.

He immediately gave her another miserable-looking smile, only half a smile this time, and immediately turned away, with his back to her, and leant up against the brown panelling.

As he leant there, she saw he was shivering all over. Dolly jumped up and put an arm around his shoulders.

"Dearest Joseph. Dear Joseph. Do come and sit down, dear," she said.

They both sat down on the window-seat together.

Dolly kept her arm round his shoulders. She could see that tears were rolling down his pale face, but he turned it half away, towards the wall, and kept wiping away the tears with his handkerchief.

94

"But what is it all, really? You must tell me what you are feeling," said Dolly.

Dolly looked painfully strained and uncomfortable. She was feeling that something had gone wrong somewhere now, that something false had crept into the situation, as they sat there on the window-seat, her arm round the shoulders of the weeping Joseph.

Joseph shook his head silently in answer to her questions, and continued shivering.

"It's no good . . .," he said, and waved his hands. Soon his shivering got worse, and sobs began to shake him. "It's no earthly use asking me what is the matter," he said roughly, gasping for breath as if he had been plunged into iced water. "I don't know myself."

After quite a long time he added, "Evelyn said some time ago (not to me) that you were in love with me, she thought."

"Well, perhaps I was some time ago. But I am not now; I haven't been for a good while."

Joseph waited a second, and then removed himself from the seat, and went over to the farther window by himself. "Why do you never tell anybody anything?" he said angrily. "You

95

always like to make out that you are on top of
the wave. That *you* can never be in need of
anyone else's help. . . ."

"Why did you never mention to me that you
were going to be married?" said Joseph, looking
at her with some sort of direct feeling in his face
now.

"Not mention it! What can you mean? You
got my letter from Albania?" cried Dolly.

"Well, good gracious, dear. That letter from
Albania! Of course I never dreamt from *that* that
you would really do it!"

"I'm sure I don't know why not," said Dolly
coldly.

"Tut!—and then why so late in the day!—
barely a month ago!"

"But if I only decided I was going to marry
a month ago!" said Dolly heatedly. "But, anyway, why all this fuss, good gracious me! You
don't want to marry me yourself! *You* are not in
love with me."

"No. . . . No. . . . I know that . . .," said
Joseph.

All of a sudden he turned sharply away from
her, began breathing in heavy long-drawn gasps

and sobs again as though he were choking over an enormous chicken-bone, and coughing.

Dolly sprang up and put her arm around his waist.

Joseph this time turned, and put his arm round her shoulder. He looked down at her; his cheeks were wet, and he gave a smile. "Darling!" he said, and there was real warmth suddenly in his voice.

As he said the word, the door handle rattled and the library door was burst open.

They both looked round with startled faces.

There stood Owen, the bridegroom, in a bowler hat, and with a travelling-rug over his arm. A look of fright came into his face as he took in the interlocked couple standing before him in the dim light, with their guilty faces, and Joseph's cheek so plainly wet with tears.

"Sorry!" he said, after a short pause.

The couple dropped apart from each other.

"But it's time to go, dear. Everybody is standing out on the doorstep waiting to bid us a fond farewell." Owen stepped instantly backwards across the threshold, and shut the door again.

97

"That has done it," said Dolly.

The door opened again, but only two inches.

"I'm sorry to interrupt, dear, but what is all this about taking a tortoise along or something or other—on board the liner with us—something —I can't understand it quite. . . . Millman handed me a biscuit tin, which she said had a tortoise inside it. . . ."

"That's all right. That's my tortoise."

"It may be your tortoise, dear, but what is it going to eat crossing over—on the boat—is what I'm thinking!"

"Why, good gracious me! (Do come in, Owen! What's the matter with you?) Surely there must be *something* on a huge big boat like that that a tortoise can eat! Good gracious me!"

"That's all very well. But I'm afraid *not*, dear, all the same."

"What! Can it not eat dried peas?"

"I'm afraid not, dear."

"At all events, it likes to eat ice wafers, I know that. And these big boats are always stacked with *them.*"

"Well . . . but if you will forgive me for doing so . . . I'm afraid I have told Millman we are *not* going to take the tortoise. They have let it loose by this time. I'm sorry. It's probably half-way over the fields to Malton by now— where, believe me, it will be very much happier than——"

"My goodness, it's perfectly insufferable!" cried out Dolly, snatching up her bag and gloves from the table.

Mrs. Thatcham poked her nose round the corner of the door.

"Oh, there you are!" she cried. "We could not think where on earth you had got to. Come along, child; everybody's waiting out on the doorstep; you'll miss your boat if you're not careful." She shooed Dolly out of the library.

On the front doorstep a huge crowd was waiting: relations, guests, and (all in a group at one side) the servants—Mad Nellie, her face flushed, and looking ready to burst with excitement and pleasure,—in spite of all her principles. The motor was ready, with baggage piled all over it, and a white satin shoe could be seen dangling from beneath a gladstone bag.

Kitty was crying, and little Evelyn was weeping quietly in the background. Red-haired Lob was standing by with a strange white paper hat on his head with long upstanding ears to it like a rabbit's; he was rolling his eyes and looking very devilish, and guarding something secret hidden under his jacket.

Out in the drive there, standing about round the motor-car, in the furious March gale, everyone felt as though they were being beaten on the back of the head and on the nose with heavy carpets, and having cold steel knives thrust up inside their nostrils, and when they opened their mouths to avoid the pain of this, big wads of iced cotton-wool seemed to be forced against the insides of their throats immediately, so that they choked, and could not draw any breath in.

In this cutting, furiously buffeting wind, amid the cries of good-bye, and bowing down before the storms of rice and confetti, the lack of high spirits on the part of the bride and bridegroom passed unnoticed. Away they drove, out of sight round the drive corner, and without wasting another moment the whole crowd made for shelter again as hurriedly as might be.

Everyone but those few who were staying in the house now took their departure.

Aunt Bella started back in her new motor to her loyal household across the bay.

Mrs. Thatcham, Kitty, little Evelyn, Lob, and the two schoolboys filtered back into the hall, one by one.

VII

In the hall they found Aunt Katie and Joseph, who had been sitting facing each other, at opposite ends of the room, in silence for the last ten minutes. Aunt Katie had taken out her little pack of patience cards and was playing "Emperor" on her basketwork patience tray.

Little Jimmy Dakin sat silently on the sofa beside her. Joseph, with legs crossed and arms folded, sat with a white face, glaring in front of him.

Suddenly a scuffle started up behind the hydrangeas.

"What did I tell you? What did I tell you? *Two men from Rugby* present at the ceremony!" chattered a voice behind the flowers, practically sobbing with nervous vexation.

There was some more sharp whispering, and

the pallid, stained white globes of the hydrangeas swayed forward dangerously in their pots.

"Children, what is the matter? Come out from behind there!"

"That fat man was Arbuthnot major!" hissed the angry voice behind the flower. . . . "All up with us now, all up! Damn you, Robert, damn you!"

Heavy breathing, and "Blast you!" shrieked Robert, tumbling out from behind the hydrangeas holding on to his left wrist, which was scarlet, and with tears pouring down his cheeks. "You are a bully!" he shouted.

"Go out of the room immediately," commanded Mrs. Thatcham, and added, quite astounded, "What extraordinary manners! Odd beings, you are! Really!" Her voice was freezing.

The boys sloped out of the room.

Mrs. Thatcham turned to Joseph. "Why not go upstairs and have a good lie down, Joseph? I would. Run along, dear boy. Go along."

"No, thank you. I'm starting for the station in ten minutes."

"Well. Why not go up even if only for ten minutes? You're not doing yourself or anybody else any good by moping round in here with a face like that, you know, child. Run upstairs. *I* should."

Joseph made no movement.

"Hetty!" shouted a deep bass voice from the top of the stairway. It was Mrs. Thatcham's Christian name.

Everyone glanced upwards.

An exceedingly elegant male figure, in a wine-coloured silk dressing-gown, which was patterned over with a design of little grey-and-white feathers, stood holding on to the banisters. It was Canon Dakin. His grey curly hair was tumbled, and his face looked pale and beautiful in the white light from the upper landing.

"I apologise for shouting down the stairway thus attired." He cleared his throat. "But a rather awkward thing has happened. I ran up to my bed-room and undressed in rather a hurry, hoping to be able to get a bath in before catching my train back to Birmingham; er—h'm—when I returned from the bathroom I found—er—apparently a woman's underclothes scattered over the bed. My own clothes I discovered had slipped down be-hind the armchair (and so, of course, had not been visible to the lady who had evidently mistaken my bedroom for hers). Er-r-r—h'm! I don't quite know. What is the best thing to do under the cicumstances? . . ."

Whilst the Canon had been speaking, Mrs. Thatcham's eye had wandered to a mysterious figure in a grey Japanese kimono with big black storks printed on it, that was lurking bashfully in the drawing-room doorway. Two long plaits of hair hung down over the shoulders. The lady had been waving a tiny white pocket-handkerchief up and down in order to attract her attention.

"But how extraordinary!" cried out Mrs. Thatcham to the Canon. "Half a moment, Bob, and I will be with you," and she hurried in and joined the lady in the drawing-room.

It was Miss Spoon, the girls' one-time governess.

"Mrs. Thatcham, it is really extraordinarily embarrassing!" those in the hall heard the latter whispering in a low voice. "I went to have a bath . . . returned to my room for a moment . . . bending down over the armchair! . . . and you see all my things in the drawers in there. . . ."

"What room are you in?" demanded Mrs.

Thatcham very loudly, and putting on her pince-nez. She could be seen, through the drawing-room doorway, staring down at the black storks on Miss Spoon's dressing-gown through her pince-nez, as though the storks and the storks alone were to blame for the whole distasteful incident.

"The lilac room, where you yourself put me," said Miss Spoon anxiously.

"Oh, Mum!" screamed out Kitty from the hall. "What did I tell you! You *would* put them all into the lilac room. I knew this would happen!"

However, when this little matter had been set right at last, Mrs. Thatcham returned to the hall again. The sun had gone down behind the trees now.

Robert had returned to the hall, and was sitting in the window-seat reading *The Captain*.

Joseph had not moved a muscle.

"Poor Aunt Katie, with nobody at all to look after you or help you with your patience!" exclaimed Mrs. Thatcham, with a glittering stare at Joseph. She began pattering roughly about the room, thumping the cushions and fluffing them out again. "Do you young men *never* think of anybody but yourselves nowadays, I wonder? To

me that seems so curious!" There was, as the saying goes, a knife-edge on her voice.

Kitty, Joseph, and Aunt Katie all turned their
heads and looked enquiringly at Mrs. Thatcham.
She was looking interested in her subject, and
seemed just about to say something further, but
no, instead she whipped an open box of chocolates off the little table beside her.

"Have a chocolate, Robert?" She went across
and handed the box to Robert in the window.

"Evelyn, a chocolate?" She waved the box at
her.

"Aunt Kate? They are so very delicious!
Joseph, help yourself, child." So saying, she put
down the chocolate-box on the table again.

Jimmy Dakin, the only person who had not
been offered a chocolate, cast his eyes down upon
the carpet, blushing hotly, and looked with very
great concentration at the Turkish arabesques
beneath his dangling feet.

A few minutes went by of general crunching
and munching.

Mrs. Thatcham ate her chocolate standing in
front of the window, her orange eyes staring out
through the little lead bars connecting the panes,

across at the rapidly tossing branches of the elm trees opposite, her neck rising very upright from her brown silk-covered shoulders.

"Excellent chocolates!" mumbled Aunt Katie with satisfaction.

"Oh, but Jimmy!" cried out Evelyn in dismay from her armchair. She had just noticed the expression on the little boy's crimson face. "Have you not been offered a chocolate?"

"Well, now! I was just waiting for somebody or other to say that!" said Jimmy with slow jocoseness, his cheeks red as fire.

"How dreadful!" cried Evelyn, and quickly handed him the chocolates, urging him to take several of them to make up for lost chances.

"Well, I had to have a laugh to myself about it, I must say!" replied Jimmy, smiling, and feeling for a chocolate. But when everyone had looked away from him again, he bent down his head and softly wiped away a tear from either eye with the lace corner of the tea-cloth beside him.

Mrs. Thatcham went and stood in front of Joseph, upon the shallow stone fender, and looked over his head away out of the window.

"You know you young men nowadays seem to mope about the place all anyhow," she said. "Never seeming to care to pull yourselves together, to stand up nice and square, or walk along properly. Or to join in with other people's fun ... don't you know what I mean?"

No one answered.

"And yet you're never lagging behindhand, I notice, when it comes to raising your voices in criticism of people old enough to be your grandmother." She pointed a finger down at Joseph. "Now, *you*, Joseph——"

"Oh, Mum!" cried Kitty from the corner.

"*You*, Joseph, have got everything you want from life: the profession you wanted, a first-rate education, all the money you want, a most devoted mother and family, and yet here you seem to be—all up against everybody! S-s-s-s-s-s-sh-sh."

In the south of France, when the *mistral* has been blowing for some time across the water, the even healthy blue complexion of the sea turns to streaks of biliousness, and to congested violet parches—a shocking sight indeed. Something of the sort had now happened upon Joseph's face.

Had it not been for the uncomfortable streaks of yellow, and the dark patches, now apparent over his neck and on the sides of his cheeks, no one would have guessed that in Joseph, during the last few minutes, a *mistral* had started up, and that deep waters were being severely ruffled.

"Nothing seems good enough for you!" said Mrs. Thatcham wonderingly. "Of course I may be very dense—but I freely confess—I utterly fail to understand it!"

Joseph, sitting back in his chair with his arms folded, raised his head and looked up into Mrs. Thatcham's eyes.

"Of course you may be very dense—that might be the reason, I suppose," he murmured thoughtfully, "that you do, as you say, so utterly fail to understand it. You can't understand why the two boys have such extraordinary manners either, can you? And then you can't understand why Mad Nellie lays the drawing-room tea incorrectly, or why the Canon and Miss Spoon come to be sharing a bedroom. You couldn't grasp how it was Millman could have been such an odd person as to lay the lunch in the library instead of the nursery! In fact, you don't really

understand anyone or anything about you, do
you? 'How odd of her!' 'How strange!' 'I may
be dense but I fail to understand it!' How many
times an hour are you obliged to confess that?"

Mrs. Thatcham stared at him as though he were
reciting the multiplication table to her all of a
sudden.

"Why not set to work," said Joseph, "by way
of a change, and determine to find out a little
about these things that puzzle you so? M-m? It
would be interesting, wouldn't it?"

Joseph's voice was as quiet when he finished
this peroration as when he began it, his face as
expressionless.

He turned his head away now, and transferred his fixed gaze slightly to the left of Mrs.
Thatcham, in the direction of the library door.
There was a silence. The lady seemed in a trance.
All gazed at the couple with—to use a vulgar
expression—their eyes fairly popping out on
stalks.

"As for where your own daughters are con-
cerned, of course, you know less than that fly
upon the ceiling," said Joseph, without turning
his head at all. "I ought not to tell you this, I

suppose," he went on reflectively, "but I'm going to. *You* didn't know, did you, that when Dolly was out in Albania last autumn she gave birth to a child out there?"

"Oh! JOSEPH!" bawled out Kitty.

Mrs. Thatcham started.

"You're mad!" she shouted, after a moment.

Joseph shook his head. "No, I'm not mad, believe me! It's true right enough, but of course *you* would be the last person to know it."

"What?"

"I say *you* would be the last person to know about it. Why! It would seem so *very* odd to you! So very curious! You would think Dolly such a 'very strange person' for doing such a thing!—that of course she must have despaired of even attempting to explain about it!"

Tears were rolling down Mrs. Thatcham's uncomprehending face.

"Oh, no need to be alarmed about it," said Joseph, watching her. "She has farmed it out with the midwife's sister in the country there. It is perfectly happy, I assure you."

Kitty sprang forward into the middle of the room and stood there uncertainly.

"What are you talking about?" shouted Mrs. Thatcham.

"Why, I am telling you that you are a grandmother. In fact, that you are doubly a grandmother—if you really want the truth! It was twins! Only I didn't like to say so. So now you have two little Albanian grandchildren, like little white mice, with pink eyes, to write letters to asking them why they haven't thanked you for the presents, and telling them how far you are from Cocklebank and Niggybottom. I must go now, or I shall lose my train. Thank you for a most delightful day." Joseph jumped up and ran away up the stairs to his bedroom.

Tears were rolling down Mrs. Thatcham's cheeks and her face looked drawn and bemused; she kept blowing her nose on a tiny little handkerchief. "But what is wrong with him? What made him speak to me like that?" she kept on and on repeating. "You can't possibly suppose . . .?" she added in a shaking voice.

"Of *course* not! Don't pay any attention, Mum! He's drunk! That's what's the matter with him!" said Kitty, putting her arm round her mamma.

"Outrageous way of talkin'," said Aunt Katie in her mild, pleasant-sounding voice. "I knew there was something a trifle fishy as soon as he mentioned that they were two little *Albanians*—with pink eyes and long white tails. Well, I said to myself, she was only in Albania five weeks all told! Rather quick work that."

"Katie!" breathed Mrs. Thatcham warningly, and indicated young Robert in the window-seat with a nod of her neatly waved grey head.

Joseph, still with his strangely impassive face, but with his heart bounding up and down in his chest with such force that he could barely draw his breath in, strode along the oil-cloth passage to his bedroom.

Here he stood in the window, and looked out over the wintry rose arches and cabbages of the now twilit kitchen garden. Somebody came and took his suit-case away, and went out again. He began to feel calmer.

He thought of what a number of times and what a number of different weathers he had stood looking out there, and thinking of Dolly, since first he had met her.

Something strange seemed to have happened

in their relationship; but he couldn't for the life of him make out what it had been. . . .

Last summer, for example, they had been inseparable, building a new summer-house together, trailing about everywhere in his boat, him teaching her how to play croquet, and so on . . . all of a sudden off she had gone to Albania, of all unheard-of places, with some stupid girl friend or other, and no sooner did she get back than, Jack Robinson! there she was engaged to be married to old Owen Bigham! Yes, there was something very strange about it all somewhere. He remembered a dinner party there had been one time down in Malton before going to the cinema.

It had been a burningly hot summer day and the dinner-table had been fixed for their party up against the open hotel window. He and Dolly had sat side by side, looking out at the sea front, which at that hour was nearly deserted. And what a melancholy, bewildered feeling stole over him as he conjured up that scene! He remembered it very clearly. Small knots of young men shop-assistants and clerks had stood about, smoking and chatting, on the pavement beneath the window. Short men they all were, he remembered, with unusually low foreheads; and many had orange or brown scarves round their necks (in spite of the August weather). Guffaws of laughter kept drifting in at the open window from these groups, cigarette smoke also, and the little men kept perpetually turning up their faces towards the dinner party. A few tousle-headed girls, with stout forms like pillar-boxes, or bolsters, wandered slowly arm-in-arm along the sea front, upon the other side of the street. The sea front, the pavement below the window, and all this side of the bay lay steeped in the late evening shadow; but the sea itself was full in the sunlight and was a startling spectacle, the whole sea-bay looking like a sheet of palest blue glass laid out gleaming underneath the pink sunset sky.

A lilac band of heat haze spread all along the horizon line, and out of this dim region a few upward-curling, clotted-cream clouds had half emerged, got caught in the pink sunset rays, and remained suspended, voluptuous-looking and completely motionless, all through dinner-time. And he remembered he had taken the white roses pinned on Dolly's shoulder for brilliant salmon-pink ones in the late sunshine; and Dolly's fascinating, melancholy face, and long plump neck beneath her straw hat, had seemed made of flame, like the glowing end of a cigarette.

They had been given fried whiting and other uneatable foods, but the wine, red burgundy, had not been at all too bad; perhaps it was on account of the latter that he had felt so extraordinarily happy—so desperate, so wild! After dinner they all set off walking to the cinema through the narrow Malton streets. Standing on the hotel steps after the meal, they observed that now all the people, the houses, the pavements and everything had turned a bright, uniform violet in the dusk. The air felt hot on their faces, and smelt strongly of syringa or heliotrope or something of the sort. Joseph and Dolly dropped behind the others. And finally lost them altogether. . . . Anyway the point was he had felt he loved her, and, though he *said* nothing, he knew that she knew this very well. She loved him too.

And yet it hadn't been love, but some depressing kind of swindle after all, it seemed.

Standing at his bedroom window by the bamboo table, and looking out at the cold March cabbages and the gravel paths, he felt that the Dolly he had walked with in the street that evening last summer was not the Dolly who had just been married this afternoon at all, and that he himself bore very little relation to the young man at Malton of that evening. And he understood that something had gone queer and awry between them since that time and the present; something was wrong, and he felt swindled. But as he was in danger of missing his train, there was no time to unravel it all just at present.

He walked off down the passage.

"'Tis better to have loved and lost than never to have loved at all," he thought with bitterness.

"Next August who shall I be taking with me in my boat?" he wondered.

A horrible feeling of depression seemed to rise up from inside him somewhere. It crept along every nerve, and kept growing deeper and deeper, like a strong physical nausea. His stomach began to turn into lead; in fact all his inside seemed to be congesting, and suffocating him with this strange, cold, heavy, physical gloom. When he reached the head of the stairway he heard the telephone bell ring down in the hall below.

"Oh it's *you*, is it, Dodo!" shouted Mrs. Thatcham into the telephone.

Hearing Mrs. Thatcham's voice, Joseph instinctively paused at the top of the stairway.

"Oh, thank you very much! Yes indeed! everything went off quite splendidly!" Mrs. Thatcham was saying down the telephone, evidently to Miss Dodo Potts-Griffiths.

Joseph's head felt heavy as a cannon-ball, and his neck as weak as worsted. He leant up against the flowered wall-paper for a moment, and rested the back of his head against the wall. He heard Mrs. Thatcham shouting cheerfully into the telephone:

"It couldn't have gone better! Yes—so dreadfully disappointing you were not able to get over. But your lampshade was very much appreciated! Yes indeed! Everybody admired it! Everybody! Quite enormously! So wonderfully clever! and so pretty and gay. S-s-s-s-sh-sh-sh. . . . Thank you very much, dear. Yes—well, of course, we had such wonderful cheerful weather for it all! The little old church looked so pretty lit up with the sunshine, don't you know—the girls' yellow frocks looked so pleasant and gay. S-s-s-s-s-s-sh-sh-sh."

118

The hall there below, Mrs. Thatcham, the whole house, and everything in it, suddenly seemed profoundly uninteresting to Joseph. It had nothing to do with him really, at all—he saw that in a flash. He looked at the scene—himself sitting there on the top stair, and the family in the hall below—as if through the wrong end of a long telescope. The buzzing in his ears got louder. A clear voice, inside his head, gave him a piece of information, above the worrying buzzing. "What you need is some brandy," said the voice. "Some brandy, yes, a good idea," he thought, and remembered that Millman had said something about it earlier in the afternoon to him. What would be the best way to get hold of Millman? On second thoughts he went along to hunt round in the dining-room himself for it.